# Road To Redemption

BACKROAD BENEFACTOR BOOK 1

**RILEY DAWSON**

STE ENTERTAINMENT, LLC

Cover Photo by CJC Photography Cover Model Kevin R Davis Cover Design RLS Images & Graphic Design

While this is a work of fiction, and the stories are all a product of my brain, along with some collaboration with a person I have come to know over the last several months. They are based somewhat in fact. The main character of this book is based on a real person, someone that I admire immensely. He faced his demons and came out on the other side. Since knowing him, I have seen him be more open and honest than many would be willing to be. He shares his story in hopes that he can help someone else find their way to a better place. He inspires me to want to do better and be better. He has given me the courage to write outside of my comfort zone and he has helped me see that there were certain people that would never make me a priority in their life, so they don't deserve to take up space in mine. So, while the situations and stories aren't real, the hero very much is. I know that he will say he's not a hero, but this is my book, and I say he is, so he can't argue. 😊 Thank you Kevin R Davis for everything you have become to me as a friend.

From Kevin R Davis-Model

My road to addiction started in my early thirties. I started having a lot of neck and upper back pain that continued to get worse and worse. For about 10 years, I did chiropractic, physical therapy, epidural injections, and nerve blocks. During that time, I was given some narcotics for pain, but the narcotics caused me to have severe stomach issues so I ended up looking for other drugs that would help relieve the pain.

I found that meth not only helped with the pain, but it made me feel so alive and productive. Eventually though, you need more and more of it, and you become less productive and can only focus on where your next high is going to come from.

Over the course of time, I had two neck surgeries, but by that point I was in full addiction, and my addiction told me that I was still in pain. I became a functioning addict for many years, but ultimately it started spiraling me down into a dark place. I was smoking and shooting meth on a daily basis.

I ended up homeless for about 6 months, crashing at friends, or sleeping in my car.

I eventually hit rock bottom when I was arrested for possession. I was face down on the ground, hands cuffed behind my back. I was locked up for 55 days. I thought my life was over, it was my worst nightmare, but little did I know, that was the best thing that could have happened to me. It caused me to finally face my issues and I couldn't hide it from the world any longer. It was what saved me. If it hadn't happened, I don't know that I would be alive today.

During those days, I was able to detox and able to do a lot of thinking about my life. I decided that I did want my life back, and I decided to do whatever it took to get there.

For once, my family knew about the secret life I had been living all those years. It felt very freeing to no longer be carrying that secret alone anymore. As part of my sentencing, I requested rehab. I was so ready to get my life back and I wanted to do whatever it took to get there. I was so tired of just existing, and I never wanted to go back to that life or go back to jail. When I was released from jail, I spent 3 months in rehab at Tuscaloosa VA Medical Center.

After rehab I decided to stay in Tuscaloosa, because I didn't know anyone there and I would have less temptations. Because I had not had sex without using for so many years, sex was my biggest trigger. I decided to remain celibate as part of my recovery and am still celibate as of today.

I also started putting a lot of my time and energy into the gym. It gave me a distraction and it made me feel good about myself again as well as transformed my body and looks. I found a job and have remained employed. I also was approached online by Golden Czermak of FuriousFotog about doing a photo shoot. That photo shoot really changed my life. It gave me even more reason to get in my best shape yet and helped tremendously with my self-esteem. It opened up so many doors for me in the modeling industry and I have had such an amazing success as a book cover model. Golden has motivated me to keep rising and to be a positive force to help others do the same.

I've also developed a very large social media following, where I am able to share my story of recovery and am hopefully able to inspire others and show them that it is possible to quit, and you can have an amazing life. It's never too late to start over. I started my recovery right before my 50th birthday, and my fifties have been my best yet!

I feel so thankful to all the people, including my family who have helped me get to where I am today. I have so much to be thankful for and I hope that I can inspire and help others who are dealing with something similar. Blessings truly do come back to you when you do for others and the joy that you get from seeing those people rise is absolutely amazing.

If you are struggling with thinking that it's not worth trying for a better life, I'm telling you that it is so worth it. You probably think it's not fun, and it's scary to give up the life that you've been living for so long. It may seem impossible at the moment, you may think that nothing will change, so why even try. Well, it isn't fun, and it is scary, and it doesn't happen overnight and you most likely will have setbacks, but it definitely can happen for you.

And to me, it's scarier to think about what would happen if you don't ever change. Make a plan and stick to it. Don't do it alone and tell others so that you are accountable and have a support system. If you need advice, find someone like me who has been there, they obviously have no room to judge.

This part of the message is not for people with an addiction though, it is for the people who love and care for someone with addiction.

I like most, did not get the help I needed until I hit rock bottom.

Rock bottom will be different for every individual. If you continue to enable someone with an addiction, you are keeping them from hitting rock bottom, and that could keep them from ever getting the help that they need.

I know that cutting someone off feels like you are abandoning them when they need you the most, but it might be the thing that actually saves their life. Helping them find help is great if they want it, but they have to be ready to make a change.

# Introduction

I've had enough.

After thirty years of living and working in a fishbowl, I'm done. More power to those who can keep on going, but this guy is burnt out.

You can call it a midlife crisis, chickening out, losing my mojo. I don't mind, because I don't really care. You see, I've done some re-evaluating of my life and I'm just not happy.

So, I've taken some photography courses on the side, got my financial ducks in a row, and now I'm going to travel around this big old country of ours to see what it has to offer.

And I'm doing it old school.

None of this GPS rubbish. I've got an atlas, a compass and a sense of adventure a mile wide. (Ok, I might have packed some extra underwear, but you get the gist). I'm going to visit the places people say they want to see before they die, and I'm going to capture snapshots of what I see there for those who'll never make it.

I'm Ray. Ray Hawthorne. Nice to meet you.

It's the end of the corporate road for me. Time to start a new journey.

The story that follows is the first stop on my journey.

# Contents


Prologue 1

1. Chapter 1 4

2. Chapter 2 14

3. Chapter 3 27

4. Chapter 4 35

5. Chapter 5 42

6. Chapter 6 54

7. Chapter 7 67

8. Chapter 8 73

9. Chapter 9 80

10. Chapter 10 87

11. Chapter 11 95

12. Chapter 12 105

13. Chapter 13 113

14. Chapter 14 124

15. Chapter 15 130

16. Chapter 16 137

17. Chapter 17 146

18. Chapter 18 152
Epilogue 156
About Author 158

# Prologue

.Ray finished loading all his camera equipment into his SUV. It was time for him to hit the road to find his new adventure. He had spent the last thirty years of his life working forty hours a week in corporate America. He had been one of the fortunate ones that had gotten a really good job right out of school and had been able to take his retirement at the age of fifty. Between his investments over the years and a small inheritance his grandfather had left him, he wasn't rich, but he was comfortable, and those investments would continue to earn money for years to come. It was time he set out and do something he had wanted to do for years. He was going to travel the country. He had bought all the best camera equipment and had taken classes at the local community college. The teacher had told him he had a natural eye for photography, so he was going to try his luck. His years in the publishing industry had given him connections to people that said they might be interested in some of the photos he took along the way.

He had specific destinations in mind, the big ones, like the Grand Canyon and Mount Rushmore, but he also wanted to travel the roads less traveled. He wanted to find the small towns and the local diners. He wanted to photograph the little boy playing with his dog and the couple sitting on their porch swing. He would photograph the fields and the forests, the mountains, and the rivers. Whatever caught his attention, he would photograph. He wasn't in it for the money, but if he sold a picture here and there, the money would just help him continue on to his next destination.

It was Monday morning, and he was leaving Los Angeles on his way toward the Grand Canyon. Although he had planned stops along the way and he was open to stopping at locations, he had never heard of too. He had no intention of having to be at any specific location anytime soon. He was using an actual paper atlas to map out his trip. He didn't want his GPS taking him on the fastest or easiest route; he wanted to pick a local highway and just cruise down it. He didn't want to be one of the many cars on the major interstates. If he found a back road going in his direction, he intended to take it.

He felt like he had spent the last thirty years inside an office, yes; it was a very elaborate office, but it still felt like a fishbowl most of the time. It had been a corner office, high up in the building, nevertheless, fishbowl. He had gotten along with his coworkers well, but he hadn't really met anyone new in years. He worked with the same people; he had lunch with the same people. Oh, not every day, but in the course of a month, he usually ended up going through the list of friends and coworkers and started back through the list again. He wanted to walk into a diner and have a chance to talk to the owner. He wanted to stop at a gas station and have a conversation with the store guy. He wanted to find the best burgers and the best beer, the best pizza, and the best donuts. He wanted to find people, every day run-of-the-mill people and spend time with them. He had sold his house, although he had retained the cabin he had in the mountains. He had a place to call home if and when he ever got tired of traveling or if he just needed to reconnect with friends in LA.

He had mapped out the general route to get out of the city and knew some of the highways to look for to head in the right direction, but mostly, he just wanted to drive and take the turn that felt right. His first destination was Joshua Tree National Park. He knew the highway that would take him there, but if he saw something interesting along the way, he would stop. There was something freeing about just having no set time schedule or a definite plan of travel. After thirty years of having to be in an office forty hours a week and having to maintain a schedule that pleased others, it was time for him to just put that all behind him and go wherever the road led him.

He would drive until he was tired and then rest. He could sleep in his car in a rest area if he had to, or he could find a cheap motel run by some elderly couple. Either way, he was going to just drive in a direction and stop when he needed to. He knew he needed to get gas often because he never knew when he would find himself on a long stretch of road with no gas station in sight. He also had a few gas cans filled in the back of his vehicle, just in case. He was going to be smart about how he did it, but he wasn't going to stress over anything. He was going to enjoy his life for as long as he possibly could.

When he left the city behind him, and it was barely a dot in his rearview mirror, he felt like he could already tell the air was cleaner. He would drive another hour or two and then find a place to get some breakfast. But not until he was in a small town with a mom and pop diner.

# Chapter 1

Ray pulled into a little town called Thousand Palms. The sign had said the population was 6,198. That sounded like the perfect place to make his first stop if they had a diner. He drove down the main road through the small town and spotted a gas station and a small diner with a sign out front that said Sally's. This looked like as good of a place as any to have breakfast. He parked his car and walked inside. The bell over the door alerted the woman behind the counter to the fact that they had a customer. She looked up like she was expecting to see someone she knew, but when she saw him, she smiled and said "Welcome to Sally's. I don't think I've seen you here before."

Ray walked up to the counter and sat down while saying, "No, I'm just passing through town. I figured I'd stop and grab some breakfast."

"Well, welcome to town. Here's a menu. Just let me know when you're ready to order. Would you like coffee?"

"Yes, please." Ray said, and then turned his attention to the menu. Sally walked over to the counter and filled a cup of coffee. She sat it next to him along with a dish with various sweeteners and creamers. She also placed a glass of ice water next to it.

Ray was trying to decide what sounded best for breakfast when he was distracted by a young boy who was sweeping the floor on the other side of the building. The boy couldn't have been more than ten or eleven at most. Ray was surprised to see him working, but then again, in a small town diner, it wouldn't be uncommon for the owner to have their kid cleaning up to help out. It was summer, so it wasn't as if the kid was skipping school.

When Sally came back toward him, he looked at her to signal that he was ready to order. "What'll you have?" she asked.

He gave her the order and then asked, "Is that your son?"

"No, he's just a boy that helps out sometimes." Sally said. She seemed like she was nervous to say too much. That made sense though. She had no idea who Ray was, and she probably didn't want him to think they were breaking any labor laws by having a minor there. She went and put his order on the spinning wheel that was between the kitchen and the main part of the diner.

Ray watched the boy finish with his sweeping and then he put the broom in a closet off to the side of the kitchen door. He made his way over to Sally and had a conversation with her that Ray couldn't hear. Then he made his way to sit in one of the booths in the back corner of the restaurant. Ray figured that his parent was probably just at one of the small shops in town and had told him to wait here. He had volunteered to sweep the floors to keep from getting bored.

Several minutes later, Sally made her way into the kitchen and came back with several plates on a serving tray. She deposited his plate of eggs and bacon in front of him and then his toast off to the side. She then walked to the booth where the boy sat and placed a large glass of milk in front of him along with a stack of pancakes and a plate of bacon. Ray was really puzzled as to what was going on. Maybe the kid didn't have parents and Sally was trying to help him out, or maybe it was none of Ray's business and he should just enjoy his breakfast.

When Sally came to clear his plates, she asked, "Is there anything else I can get you?"

"I'd like a refill on my coffee and a little information if you don't mind." He said, pushing his cup closer to her on the counter. Ray could tell she was a little apprehensive of what his question was going to be, most likely because she seemed to not want to share many details of who the kid was. When she came back with the coffee pot, Ray said. "I'm planning to be in the area for a few days. I'm going to be taking some photos at the national park. Is there a hotel or bed-and-breakfast anywhere nearby?"

That seemed to make her a little more at ease. "Well, two blocks up, there's Maude's boarding house, or if you want an actual motel, there's one about ten miles up the road closer to the park."

"Thanks, Maude's sounds perfect." Ray said.

If Sally was curious as to why he would pick the location that was further away from his destination, she didn't say anything. "Maude's a bit of an odd duck, if you know what I mean. She runs a bed-and-breakfast, but she's always a little stand offish with strangers. Tell her I sent you and she should be okay." Sally said.

He paid his tab and took one more look at the little boy. He had almost completely cleared his plate. It had been a large helping. Ray wondered if it had been a while since the kid had a meal. He had never gone hungry in his life, but he had gone to school with some kids that didn't have much to eat at home. He always used to ask his mom to pack an extra sandwich so that he could give it to his friend Bobby.

Ray found the house that had a sign out front that simply said "Maude's" on it and parked his car on the road in front of the house. Before he could make it all the way up the driveway, the front door opened and a woman who looked to be in her sixties came out onto the large porch. "You the one Sally called me about?"

"That would be me." Ray said, giving his best smile. "I was hoping to rent a room for a few days."

"She says you're on your way to Joshua Tree. Why ain't you staying at the hotel up the road a piece?"

Oh, this woman had so much charm in a weird 'I don't like you,' sort of way. "Well, I just like small towns, I guess. I lived in LA for years and I'm just ready to not be in the hustle and bustle."

"How many days you stayin'?" she asked.

Ray thought about that. How many days was he staying? He would only need a few days to take all the photos he would want at the national park, but this town, and especially that little boy had him curious. "I'd like to start with a week, and take it from there, if that's agreeable to you."

"Two hundred for the week." she said. The way she said it had come across like she thought maybe he would balk at the price, but that was way cheaper than any hotel would be. "It includes breakfast and I always have a pot of coffee on. You're welcome to take some. Your room has its own bathroom, so you don't have to share."

"I'll take it!" Ray said. He had put a fair amount of cash in his wallet because one never knew when you would need cash over credit. He pulled out his wallet and pulled out two one hundred-dollar bills. He was pretty sure Maude didn't have a card reader.

She took the money, held each bill up to the sunlight, and then tucked it into her bra. "I'll show you your room." she said, waving her hand for him to follow.

Maude had a wonderful, older two story home. Ray complimented her on how well it was taken care of. She had pictures all around the house of her and what Ray assumed to be her husband and children. "Are these your kids?" he asked.

Maude took one of the pictures from a shelf and said, "That there is my husband, Bill, Lord rest his soul. This here is Bill junior; this is Betsy, and this is Nick." She had pointed to each person in turn as she said their name. She pointed at another picture on the wall that had several more people in it and gave the name of each spouse and grandchild and which of her children they belonged to. Ray knew he wouldn't keep it all straight, but he took it all in just the same. "Do any of them live close by?" he asked when she had named everyone.

"No, Nick and Betsy live in Florida and Bill junior lives in Detroit. They all moved for jobs. There aren't a lot of jobs in a small town like this." Maude said. "They visit when they can." The way she said that gave Ray the opinion that it wasn't nearly as often as Maude wished it would be.

She showed him to his room and told him to make himself to home. If he needed anything to let her know. Ray decided that instead of heading to the national park today, he'd check out this small town. After all, his motto for life now was to take the road less traveled, so it would be nice to just stroll around and maybe meet a few people. He headed back downstairs and found Maude in the living room; she was watching some game show on television. "I'm going to go for a walk. Is my car parked okay or do you need me to move it somewhere else?" he asked.

"No, it's fine, we don't get a lot of traffic on this side street." Maude said. "If you stop by Sally's, you tell her that I'm bringing my potato salad to the picnic on Saturday so she can make something else."

"I'll do that." Ray said with a smile. He got the sense that there was a story there, but he also had a feeling Maude wouldn't be the one to tell it. He walked out of the house and looked around, trying to decide which way to go first. He decided to go the opposite direction that he had come from. He would circle around a few blocks and see what was there. Eventually he would end up back at Sally's since it was the only place to eat in town. It would take him a few days to exhaust the menu at the diner and Maude had offered him breakfast each day, but if he got the desire for something different; he could always take a drive out of town or stop somewhere on his way to Joshua Tree.

He had gone a few blocks when he came to a small park with a few swings and slides. There were picnic tables and those grills that were on a pole coming out of a cement pad. He spotted the small boy that he had seen earlier in the day. He was sitting on a swing with a scrawny-looking dog a few feet away from him. It looked like the dog wanted to approach the boy, but he wasn't sure. The dog was probably a stray and didn't get much human interaction. Ray was close enough to hear the boy, but he was behind him, so the child didn't know he was there.

"Hey, boy." the child said. "You hungry?" He pulled out a napkin and unwrapped a couple of pieces of bacon and a pancake. He held a strip of bacon out toward the dog and the animal tentatively sniffed and then took a step and sniffed again. The boy remained very still, so he didn't spook the animal. Eventually, the dog got close enough that he could grab the other end of the bacon. He took it and ran a few steps back, watching to make sure the child didn't try to grab him. He chewed down the bacon rapidly and came tentatively back for more. This time, the boy held out the pancake. The dog repeated the same procedure, but eventually took the pancake and laid down to eat it. When he was done, the boy held out the remaining piece of bacon and the dog seemed a little less timid when he took it. He was starting to trust that the boy wasn't going to hurt him.

Ray wasn't sure if the dog had been abused, so he was timid or if he just hadn't been around many people. After the dog had stepped back, Ray stepped a step closer to the boy. He didn't want to scare either of them away. "Is that your dog? He looks like he's a good one."

The boy turned at the sound of the man's voice. He remembered seeing him at the diner earlier. "No, I just feed him. He doesn't have anyone to feed him so if I have extra, I bring him some." the boy said.

"That's really nice of you. I bet he'll be your dog in no time. Dogs can tell when they have a good person taking care of them." He smiled at the boy and then said, "My name is Ray, what's yours?

"I'm Lance." he said. "You really think he will want to be my dog someday?"

"I do." Ray offered, "I'd be glad to help you get some food to bring to him. I'm going to be in town for a few days and I bet by the time I leave we can get him to come to you."

"Really, you'd help me?" the boy exclaimed. It seemed to Ray that maybe the boy didn't have a lot of people that kept their promises to him in his life. He would befriend the child and see if there was anything else he could help him with while he was in town.

"Sure, I'll get some things from the grocery store when I'm in town and I'll bet we'll have him friendly in no time." Ray promised.

"Thanks Mister." The boy was beaming with a huge smile.

"Nope, if we're going to be friends and work together to get you a dog, you have to call me Ray."

"Okay, Ray, thanks!"

The dog had gone several feet away now that there wasn't any food to attract him closer. Ray sat on the swing next to Lance. He didn't want to pry too much into the boy's life until he had a chance to make him feel more comfortable, so he asked, "Since I'm new here, what is there that's fun to do around here?"

"Well, not a lot really." Lance began. "We don't have enough kids to do a sports team. During the summer lots of kids go to camp and stuff too, so there's less of us."

"Do you go to camp?" Ray asked. He was going to try to stick with questions about things that Lance had offered up rather than seeming to pry.

"I used to." Lance said. "Not this year though."

Ray got the feeling that the reason for that was more than the boy would be willing to share right now, so he didn't press it. "You don't need a whole team to bat a ball around or play some catch. You can shoot hoops too if there's a basketball net anywhere nearby."

"I don't have a basketball. There's a hoop down at the school. I play sometimes on recess when we're in school." Lance said.

"Well, you'll have to show me where it is sometime." Ray offered. "We can play a game."

"You have a basketball?" Lance asked, wide eyed.

"I can get one." Ray said.

"That would be awesome."

Ray was pretty sure he had made a new friend and over time, he would find out the rest of his story. When they parted ways, Ray decided to go back towards Maude's. He was going to pick up his car. He had several items he needed to buy, and he couldn't carry them all. Heck, he wasn't even sure he could get them all in this small town. He'd drive wherever he had to to get them though, even if it meant he had to go back towards LA to find a town big enough to carry a basketball and all the things needed to win over a scared timid scruff of a dog.

Fortunately, he was able to find everything within a couple of hours, although he did have to go to a larger town twenty miles away to find a basketball. He had them all in his vehicle, but it was getting close to dinner time when he got back to town, so he pulled up to Sally's to grab a bite before heading to Maude's for the night.

He stepped into the diner and saw Lance rolling silverware into napkins and putting the band around them to hold them together. He looked up from his work and waved, a large smile on his face. Ray waved back.

"Looks like you made a friend," Sally said handing him the menu.

"I was out for a walk today and I ran into Lance. We talked a little, it's no big deal really." Ray said. He put his head down to study the menu, hoping that Sally wouldn't ask anything more. He could tell that Sally was protective of the boy. He wasn't sure why. He didn't want her to think that he had any ill intent toward the child, and he got it. He was the stranger in town. They had no way of knowing if he was friend or foe. So far it didn't seem like Lance had any parents, or if he did, they weren't very present in his life. Ray was glad that the kid had people in town who watched out for him if his parents didn't take the responsibility.

He ate his meal, but he set aside the dinner roll that had come on a separate plate. He rolled it into his napkin and tucked it into his backpack. He would try to sneak it to Lance. He had actual dog food and treats so that the boy could try to win over the dog, but he also figured that the boy would see the dinner roll as a gesture of solidarity from him in the battle to win the dog.

By the time he was done eating, Lance had finished his job and was walking toward the door. Sally was back in the kitchen, so he tilted his head a couple of times to signal Lance to come over. He reached into his backpack and pulled out the dinner roll. He handed it to Lance, keeping it below the level of the counter. He wasn't sure if the boy wanted others knowing he was feeding the dog or not, so he wanted to try to keep it on the down low.

Lance took the balled up napkin and realized that there was something in it. He looked up at Ray and Ray gave him a conspiratorial wink. Lance's face lit up with a huge smile and then he ran out the door.

When Sally came back out of the kitchen, she had a suspicious look on her face, but she didn't say anything. Ray paid his tab and headed back to Maude's. He didn't see Lance anywhere, even though he had taken a route that would take him past the small park. He had no idea where the boy lived, but he hoped he had a home to go to.

When he arrived at Maude's he wasn't really tired, it wasn't that late yet. He figured he could go upstairs and watch the television in his room, or he could stream something on his tablet, or he could sit and talk with Maude. The latter sounded like the best idea. After all, his goal had been to meet people and have conversations with them. He had made headway with Lance, he was pretty sure the jury was still out with Sally, but he could try to talk to Maude.

He found her in the living room of the large house. She had the television on and again was watching a game show. This time it was Jeopardy. Ray stood back and listened as Maude answered clue after clue correctly. This was one smart woman even though she sort of came across as a country hick when you talked to her. He didn't want to startle her, so he bumped into the wall a little as he stepped into the room. She looked up at him, so he said, "Hey Maude, do you mind if I watch with you for a little while. I'm just not ready to go to bed yet I guess."

"No, make yourself to home." she said, turning back to her show.

Ray listened for several more questions. Maude didn't get every single one right, but she got way more than he would have. "How do you know so many of these?" he asked.

"Oh, I don't know, I read a lot I guess." Maude said. When the show was over, Maude turned it off and said, "Tell me about you, Ray."

"Well, I worked for thirty years at a major corporation in Los Angeles. I just retired a few weeks ago. I decided I wanted to travel the country and take pictures of things that I saw and liked. I'm going to take some that will probably sell to travel magazines or things like that, but mostly I just want to see the country." Ray said.

"Can you take a picture of me before you leave?" Maude asked.

"Sure."

"I want to send it to my kids. I can get copies at the drugstore." Maude explained. "I don't get many pictures taken and I'm afraid my grandkids will forget what I look like."

"I'd be glad to help you get pictures for them Maude." Ray's mind began to whirl with the possibilities. He was sure that Maude didn't really know much about the internet, but maybe he could help her find a way to connect with her family by way of video chat. Even if she got a smartphone, she could do that. He was sure that her children would have the technology. He would have to check into what options were available in a small town like this one.

They chatted for a while longer when Maude said, "I'm going to make some chamomile tea before I go to bed, would you like a cup?"

"Sure, that sounds great." It had been years since Ray had had any tea. He was more of a coffee man, but he liked the simple life that this woman lived and if she wanted to share her tea with him, he wasn't going to turn her down. She was probably very lonely. Even in a town where everyone knew each other if you didn't have actual family, you sometimes felt like you were on the outside.

By the time the tea was brewed and consumed, Ray had a full plan in place. He wasn't sure that Maude would really want a cell phone. She had a landline phone on the wall, and she might consider a cellphone a pain because she could lose it if she had to carry it around all the time. He was pretty sure that a computer was beyond her technology skills. But, a simple tablet, if connected to the internet with the right apps installed, would make it possible to video chat with her family. He decided that tomorrow he would find out from Sally what the Wi-Fi situation was in the area and take it from there. When he went to his room, he pulled out his own tablet and did some research into a tablet that would be simple for Maude to use and would give her the only thing that really mattered to her, a way to chat and exchange pictures with her children. He found the perfect one and put it in his cart. If there was available Wi-Fi, he would make the purchase.

When he went to bed, he felt satisfied with what he had accomplished on his first day in Thousand Palms. Hopefully, tomorrow would prove to be just as productive.

# Chapter 2

When Ray got up the next morning, he went downstairs to find Maude in the kitchen working on breakfast. "There's fresh coffee in the pot, help yourself." she said. "Breakfast is almost done, take a seat."

Ray liked Maude's straightforward no nonsense approach to life. He poured himself a cup of coffee took a sip and sat at the table. "Breakfast smells really good and this coffee is perfect."

"Well, I suppose I'm no Sally's, but I think I make a good breakfast." Maude said.

Ray seriously needed to figure out what the deal was between Maude and Sally. There seemed to be some sort of tension there, although he hadn't sensed any from Sally. She had freely recommended Maude's as a good place to stay and had even told him to tell Maude she sent him. So, it didn't seem like there was any animosity on the younger woman's behalf. Maybe the younger woman had offended Maude at some point.

When Maude had served the meal and sat across from him at the table, he asked, "When I was out walking yesterday, I met a young boy. He said his name was Lance, do you know anything about him?"

"Well, I know who he is." Maude said. She hesitated for a minute, she wasn't sure what all she should say, but eventually she continued, "He's a good kid, had a rough time of it the last six months or so."

"Rough time in what way?" Ray asked.

"Well, his daddy was a Marine." Maude began.

"Was?" Ray asked. Had the man been discharged, or had ne not survived?

"He was killed in action, somewhere in the middle east, I don't know where exactly." Maude said. "Lance's momma took it pretty hard, she hasn't been the same since. I don't really see her around town at all anymore."

"Lance said he used to go to summer camp and stuff, but he couldn't go this year." Ray said. "I would think his mother got a settlement of some kind. Or a pension, the military would have some sort of compensation I would think. Does she work that you know of?"

"She used to, oh it wasn't some high paying job, but she did okay. She was the manager at the store in town." Maude said. "But when she got the news, she just kind of stopped existing, if you know what I mean?"

"Do you think she treats Lance okay?" Ray asked, as much as he would hate to have to step in, he wouldn't hesitate to call child protective services if he was being abused or neglected.

"I don't think she's mean to him or anything." Maude said, "At least I haven't ever heard any rumor of it. I don't think she's always really active most days. But I think his needs are met. I guess I don't really know for sure though."

Ray didn't push for any more information; Maude wouldn't likely know much more about it anyway. He would try to do some more investigating without seeming like the creepy guy who was stalking a little kid. When he was done with his breakfast, he helped clear the table and then he decided to drive around a bit and see if he saw Lance anywhere, he wanted to give him some of the stuff that he had gotten for the dog and make sure that the boy knew that it was okay to come and get more from him whenever he needed it.

He found Lance in the same park as he had been the day before. Ray got a feeling that he probably hung out there a lot. He was sitting in the same swing and the dog was about fifteen feet away munching on a waffle. Ray grabbed a bag of treats, the bowl he had bought and filled it with one can of dog food and walked slowly toward Lance. He didn't want to startle either the boy or the dog. The dog did see him coming first though and perked up his head, that made Lance aware that someone was there, so he turned to see who it was. When he saw his newfound friend, he said, "Hi, Ray!"

The dog had finished its food, so it had taken several steps back towards the woods at the edge of the park. The dog looked pretty scrawny; it was likely that the only real food it got was whatever Lance had been able to sneak to it. It probably scavenged a trash can here and there or found things in dumpsters in town, but it definitely wasn't getting fed properly. "Hey Lance," Ray greeted the boy. "I brought some stuff so that we can work on getting you a dog. Let's put this bowl of food right over here. We don't want it too close, or he won't come and get it, but we want it close enough that he has to get a little out of his comfort zone if he wants the food." Ray sat the bowl about eight feet away from where they would be sitting. It was closer than the dog usually sat with the food he grabbed from Lance, but he had been close enough to grab food out of the boy's hand, so he already wasn't very afraid of Lance. He had chosen a bowl that wouldn't be easy for the dog to just pick up and carry away. It was large enough and heavy enough that a dog the size of this one likely wouldn't have the ability to get enough of it in his mouth to run away with it.

Ray sat on the swing next to Lance and they both watched the dog begin to sniff the air. He started walking back and forth looking at the bowl and sniffing but not getting any closer. "He's not going to come get it." Lance said sadly.

"Oh, he will, but we may have to coax him a little bit, especially with me here, he doesn't know if he can trust me yet." Ray explained. "He's already gotten a little comfortable with you, but I'm a stranger. But I think I can earn his trust for both of us." Ray opened the bag of treats and pulled out one of the pieces of jerky. He did his best to toss it right in front of the dog's nose, but about a foot away. When it hit the ground near him, the dog startled and acted like he might run, but in the end, he just started sniffing the air. It finally took the step necessary to be able to grab the treat. Ray tossed another piece about two feet closer to the bowl. The dog was too busy eating its current treat to be very bothered by the thump the new one made when it landed on the ground. He took the two steps toward it when he had finished the first. This time, Ray hesitated a bit before throwing another one. He wanted to see if the dog immediately began its retreat, or if it stayed hoping for more. When it just sat and looked toward them as if waiting to see what they would do, Ray tossed another one. This one ended up about half way between where the dog was and where the bowl of food sat on the ground.

The dog tentatively walked over and took the treat. He stayed where he was and ate it but didn't approach the food dish right away. He stretched his neck as far forward as he could sniffing the scent of the food. Ray had chosen soft food because he wasn't sure exactly what the dog's health would be like. He had chosen something that was high in nutrition and was soft and moist. It would be the easiest to digest if he did have poor health. If they could ever get him to trust them, Ray would need to find out if there was a vet nearby. He didn't see any outward signs that gave Ray any concern, but he would like to be sure that things were okay.

Finally, after standing for several minutes sniffing and looking at the food and then at the humans, the dogs hunger won out and he took the additional steps needed to get to the bowl of food. Lance quickly looked towards Ray with the biggest smile on his face. Ray put a finger over his lips to signal that the boy should stay quiet, if the dog didn't have any reason to fear them, he would likely eat his fill. If he got startled, it would be more difficult to get him to be willing to try again.

They both watched as the dog cleaned the entire bowl of food and then looked up at the two of them for a long moment as if he were trying to assess their motive or maybe it was his way of saying thanks for the food. He didn't race away; he slowly made his way back into the shade of the trees and laid down. A thought occurred to Ray; he wasn't sure that the dog had access to clean drinking water. There would likely be a pond or river where he could find water, but that might not be clean water. "Stay here for a minute, Lance, I'll be right back." He got up and slowly walked over to the dish and picked it up. The dog carefully watched his every move. He took it to the faucet that was on a pole near the barbeque area of the park. He rinsed out the bowl the best he could and then filled it with water. It wasn't super cold, but after running it long enough to clean the dish, the temperature had dropped some. He thought about just leaving the faucet running at a slow stream, he would have to see if there were many people that came to the park because it would likely get turned off pretty quickly if there were. He didn't go far with the bowl of water, if they did decide to leave the faucet on at some point, he wanted the dog to associate getting clean water from that part of the park. It also made it so that the dog didn't have to come close to them to get the water. An animal would go through a lot to get food, but if water was easily available, even if it wasn't clean water, the dog would drink it rather than having to work for it here.

Ray walked back over to the swings and sat with Lance. "I have lots of food and treats for the dog. If you ever need any, you just come and find me. I'm staying at Maude's. In fact, I'll see if she minds me leaving some in a box on the porch or something in case I'm not around."

"Okay, thanks, Ray." Lance said. "I really hope he can be my dog someday."

"Do you think your parents will be okay with you having a dog?" Ray asked. He wasn't going to give away the fact that he knew about Lance's dad. He wanted the boy to tell him about it whenever he was ready. He gestured for Lance to look because the dog was happily trotting over to the bowl for the water, no human threat made it easy for him to move towards it quickly.

"I don't have a dad," Lance began, "well, not anymore. He was a soldier and he died."

"I'm really sorry to hear that, Lance." Ray said sincerely. "I bet you're proud of him for being a soldier though.

"Yeah, it was hard sometimes because he couldn't always come home much, but I knew what he was doing, and I always knew that he was keeping everyone safe." Lance stated.

"What about your mom?" Ray asked. He was trying to keep everything simple, like they were just two guys hanging out and talking. If his mother wasn't around much or was going through some issues because of his father's death, Ray didn't want him to feel like he was giving away incriminating information.

"She's been really sad, since my dad died." Lance said.

"Yeah, I bet." Ray responded. He didn't say anything more, he wanted to give Lance time to share or not share whatever he felt comfortable with. He would listen to anything the boy wanted to tell him and he would try to find out more by observation and conversations with others in town.

"She sometimes doesn't feel like making dinner or stuff, so that's why I go to Sally's" Lance finally admitted. "Sally's my aunt so she lets me eat dinner there. I try to sweep the floors or do the silverware or stuff because she always gives me all the food I want for free."

"I bet she would do that just because she's your aunt," Ray stated. "But I'm sure she appreciates you helping out."

"My dad always taught me that if someone does nice stuff for you, you should do stuff for them too."

"Your dad sounds like he was a really great guy." Ray said.

"Yeah." Lance said softly.

They didn't talk for a while, they both just watched the dog and thought over the things that were going on in their own heads. Finally, the dog had its fill of the water and it laid down again, still in the shade, but not as far away as it had gone before. It was already starting to realize that these two people meant it no harm. Hopefully Ray could earn Lance's trust just as much.

"Well, it looks like he's happy for now." Ray began, "have you thought of a name for him?"

"No, I didn't want to jinx it by giving him a name until he's my dog for sure." Lance said.

"That makes sense, but I'm pretty sure he will be yours before you know it." Ray offered. "I'm getting kind of hungry, how about you?"

Lance was quiet as if he didn't know what to say.

"Can I buy you lunch at Sally's and then maybe you can show me around town. I'm new here and you know all the good places." Ray said. "It would be only fair if I buy your lunch if I'm going to ask you to take your afternoon showing me around."

"Okay." Lance said. "That's a good deal."

"Well, I have my car here, but I don't know if you are supposed to ride with strangers." Ray began. "I wouldn't want to get you into any trouble or anything. I can just leave my car here and we can walk to Sally's."

Lance didn't say anything, he just got up and started walking in the direction of the main street.

"So, you say there's a basketball hoop by the school?" Ray asked.

“Yeah.” Lance responded. “They don’t have a fence around it so people are allowed to use it anytime. It’s not like a hole basketball court, just a small cement part with one hoop.”

“Well, maybe we can shoot some hoops there sometime.” Ray offered. “When I picked up the basketball, I also got some baseball stuff. I know you said that there isn’t enough people for a whole game, but we could still play catch.”

“That would be fun.” Lance said. They were approaching the diner, so the conversation stopped long enough for them to walk through the door.

When the door opened, Sally looked up, she looked surprised to see Lance, but was even more surprised when she saw who walked in behind him. Ray tried to act like it was no big deal and followed Lance to the booth the boy usually sat in.

When they were seated, she walked over to the table with raised eyebrows that only Ray could see. “Hi, Sally.” he began, “Lance here is going to be my tour guide showing me around town today, so I figured the least I could do is buy him lunch.”

“Yeah, Ray’s trying to help me get a dog.” Lance said excitedly. Ray cringed; he wasn’t sure how Sally would feel about that part.

“If you mean that scraggly looking thing that’s always trying to get into my trash cans, more power to you.” Sally said.

“Ray bought treats and food and a bowl and everything.” the boy said.

“Oh, really?” Sally asked. “Lance, why don’t you go wash your hands, I know you’ve been playing in the park.”

Ray had absolutely no doubt that Sally was sending the boy away so that she could have a private talk with him. So, as soon as Lance was out of ear shot, he started his explanation, “Look, I’m sure you’re wondering what my motive is, and I’ll be honest, I have one. I have seen Lance in here a few times and at the park a couple of times. He’s told me a little bit of his story, I know his dad died in the military, I know his mom hasn’t been the same since. I know you are his aunt and I know he seems to need a friend right now. He says most of the kids his age are off to camp. I’m not trying to do anything weird; I'm just trying to be his friend while I am here and maybe help him get a dog that will be his friend after I leave."

Sally stood there and just looked at him for a long time as if she were trying to determine how much truth was in his little speech. Finally, she said "Okay, but don't hurt that boy when you leave, He's had enough to deal with already."

"I won't." Ray promised. By that time, Lance was coming back to the table, so the adults dropped that conversation for now. Ray had no doubts that Sally would be keeping an eye on things and that was fine with him. It was obvious that Lance needed someone to watch out for him.

"Do you know what you want, or do you need a menu?" Sally asked. "The special is the chicken tenders with mac and cheese."

"I want the special." Lance said without hesitation. "And chocolate milk."

"Make that two." Ray agreed.

"Chocolate milk for you too or something else?" Sally asked.

"Chocolate milk will be fine." Ray responded.

Sally walked toward the window into the kitchen and put the order tag on the spinner and then went to get two glasses of chocolate milk.

"So, I was thinking, maybe when we leave, we take the long way around to the park. Which ever way you want to go is fine, and then when we get back to the park, maybe we can play a little catch, and see if your dog is back for more food."

"Yeah, that sounds good" the little boy said happily.

"You know, you're going to have to think of a name for him, we can't keep calling him the dog." Ray said.

"I was thinking Lucky, because if he ends up my dog, I'll be lucky to have him." Lance stated.

"That's a good name." Actually, Ray wasn't completely positive that the dog was a male, so it would probably be good that Lance didn't want to give it a name that was all male. Lucky could go either way really, especially with the boy's explanation of why he picked that name.

When Sally brought their food, Ray remembered what he was supposed to tell her. "I was supposed to tell you that Maude is bringing her potato salad to the picnic, so you can pick something else to make."

Sally just shook her head and said, "That woman."

"It sounded like there was a story there, but I wasn't about to ask Maude." Ray said.

"Oh, there's a story, believe me." Sally began. "It was fifteen years ago; we had only been living here for about six months. The town has a Founder's Day picnic every year. So, I made potato salad, everyone loves potato salad, right?"

At Ray's nod, she continued. "Well, what I didn't know was that Maude makes a huge batch of potato salad, every year, it's like her specialty or something. I've never again taken potato salad in all the years since, but whenever she gets a chance, she reminds me that she brings the potato salad." Sally was still shaking her head.

"Maude seems like a bit of an odd duck, but she's really smart and I'm sure she's lonely with her family all moved away." Ray said.

"Oh, I'm sure she is." Sally agreed. "We don't often get people in town that want to stay at her place, most want to go to a regular hotel. She opened up the boarding house or bed and breakfast or whatever you want to call it because she was just rattling around in that house all alone. But I don't know that it's helped with so few wanting to stay."

"I was wondering, does the town have any kind of Internet service?" Ray asked.

"We have it." Sally said. "Mostly the younger generation use it. Why? Are you needing it? I can give you our password if you want to use it while you're here."

"No, I was wondering more for Maude's sake." Ray stated.

"I don't think she would think she has any use for it to be honest." Sally said.

"Well, I thought maybe if she had a very simple tablet, with a video call program installed she could stay in touch with her family. She said she's afraid her grandkids won't even know what she looks like. She asked me to take pictures, which I will still do, but I thought that might be a more long term solution. And if she does get set up with Wi-Fi it might give an added pull for people to want to stay there."

A group of people had walked in and sat down at another booth, so Sally excused herself and went to get them started. When she came back, she said. "You know, I think that's a really nice thing you want to do for Maude. I think that the only thing she would use it for is the video calls, but I think she would be so happy to have it. For no more than she would need, she could tap into the Internet around here for about ten dollars a month."

"Do you know how to get in contact with her family?" Ray asked. "I'd want to make sure they know she's set up."

"I have her son's number at home." Sally said, "I kept it in case I ever needed to contact them if something happened to Maude. I'll copy it down tonight and have it with me the next time you stop by."

"Thanks, I'd appreciate that." Ray said.

"I've got to get back to work, but you two let me know if you need anything." Sally said.

"Thanks, we will." Ray looked at Lance who had been quietly eating away at his lunch. He was wrapping a chicken tender into his napkin. Ray wasn't sure why, so he asked, "Are you too full to eat that?"

"Um, no, I um, just wanted to save it for Lucky." Lance sort of mumbled.

"No, Lance, I have lots of food for Lucky." Ray said. "You eat your fill. Besides, it's best to get Lucky used to food that's made for him. It's healthier that way. Sometimes human food isn't made with all the same stuff a dog would need. If you can, you should try to eat it."

“Okay.” Lance agreed. He unwrapped the chicken and took a bite.

When the entire thing was gone, Ray said, “Now, I don’t mean you can’t ever feed him scraps of your food. It’s okay to give him something if you honestly can’t eat it. But the more we can get him to like dog food and expect to be fed it on a regular basis, the less he’s going to be looking for human food in people’s trash cans. If you want people to like your dog, he has to learn manners. Now, I know he’s not going to be able to be trained to do everything right away, but the more we can get him to start thinking that you’re going to give him dog food every day, he’ll think he needs to find his own food less. You see what I mean?”

“Yeah, that makes sense,” the boy agreed.

When Sally placed the bill on their table, Ray noticed that she had only charged him for one special, but he had invited Lance to lunch and he intended to pay for both meals so he doubled the amount and then added a tip accordingly and left it on the table as they walked out.

“Which way should we go Lance?” Ray asked. “Show me around town.”

Lance thought about it for a minute, and then he said, “Let’s go this way.” He started in the general direction of the park, but definitely not a direct route. After a few blocks, he made a turn and said, “This is my school, see right there’s the basketball hoop.”

“Yeah, that’s a nice big space to play in.” Ray stated. “Like you said, not a full court, but there’s enough room to dribble and line up a shot.”

“We sometimes play horse or cat or whatever on recess, but we usually run out of time.” the boy said.

“Well, maybe we can meet down here tomorrow, that way I’ll have the ball in my car.” Ray said. “Do you like going to school?”

“It’s okay.” Lance said. “I think I have to go back to fifth grade again though.” The boy seemed to be depressed about that fact.

“Yeah?” Ray said. “You probably had a tough year last year with your dad and all.”

"Um hmm." Lance said.

"Did they say you have to do fifth grade again, or that you might have to do it again?" Ray asked.

"They said that I could go to sixth grade if I can study and take some test." Lance said solemnly.

"Well, that might not be so bad." Ray encouraged. "And if you do have to do fifth grade again, you'll already know most of the stuff so it should be a breeze." He hoped that he could help the boy see that this wasn't the end of the world.

"I know, but I won't have any friends in my class anymore."

Now Ray got it. It wasn't at all about the schoolwork having to be redone, it wasn't about any kind of embarrassment over being held back. Most likely everyone would understand why that had happened. It was about the one thing that would matter most to a kid who had so little in the way of relationships and connection in his life. "Did they give you the stuff to study, or tell you how to get it?" Ray asked.

"Yeah, my teacher said that my mom could contact her and set me up with a person that would help me." Lance said. He didn't continue, but Ray had a feeling that the rest of the story was that he had told his mom and for whatever reason, it hadn't been followed through on. Ray really wanted to figure out what was going on with the boy's mother. He could understand grief and loss, he had lost people. What he couldn't understand was why her son had seemingly been forced to the outside of her life.

"Well, maybe it's still not too late and you can work on it." Ray said.

The boy was kind of hanging his head, like he didn't really think there was much hope that it would happen, but he mumbled, "Maybe."

Ray would do whatever he could to check into the situation and see if the boy could move on to sixth grade with his friends. He realized that he really didn't have much of a say in the matter, but this was a small town, and Sally was the boy's aunt, so maybe he could find out something through her if Lance's mother wasn't going to be helpful.

Finally, after standing there and seeming to process whatever thoughts were going on in his head, Lance started to make his way down the road again. When they got to a gray house on a corner, Lance said "My friend Tom lives there, he's at camp right now though."

A woman stepped out on the porch and said "Hello, Lance. Tom is still at camp if you're looking for him."

"I know Mrs. Murphy; I was just showing my friend Ray here around town." the boy explained. "He's new and he doesn't know anybody."

The woman came out on the sidewalk to greet him and said, "Did you move here, I hadn't heard of any new residents."

"No, I'm just staying here for a little while, I'm staying over at Maude's." Ray explained. "I'm going to be taking some photos up at Joshua Tree and I wanted to stay someplace a little more homey than a hotel chain." He reached out his hand and added, "It's a pleasure to meet you."

She shook his hand and said, "It's nice to meet you too. Where did you and Lance meet?"

Ray liked that the people of the town all seemed to be concerned for Lance. If his mother wasn't fully functional, for whatever reason, it was nice that others were watching out for him. "Well, we saw each other at Sally's but then we actually met in the park. I was walking around trying to familiarize myself with where everything was. Lance offered to be my tour guide for today." He wanted to put the woman's mind to rest so he added. "We started by having lunch at Sally's and so far, I've seen the school and now I've met you. I think my tour guide is doing an excellent job of showing me the highlights of the city."

The woman blushed a little at the compliment but seemed to be okay with him being with Lance since they had been together at Sally's. "Oh, yes, well enjoy your tour then." She turned to Lance and added "Tom will be back in two weeks, on Friday."

"Yes, ma'am." Lance gave a nod of his head. They moved on down the street again.

# Chapter 3

By the time they arrived back at the park, Ray had seen most of one quarter of the town. Lance had pointed out a church, although he said there were two more in other parts of town. Ray asked if Lance ever went to church, and the boy said that they used to go sometimes. They had passed the post office and the small grocery store that Ray had stopped at the day before. They had zig zagged up and down whatever streets Lance felt were important for Ray to see.

When they got to the park, Ray noticed that Lucky was near the faucet, lapping at the water that was forming a small puddle on the cement. He was putting his head under the small trickle that Ray had left coming out. Ray wasn't sure how long others would be okay with that, but he figured with a lot of the kids from town being at camp the park wasn't getting used as much as it normally would. When Lance looked at him, Ray tilted his head in the direction of the faucet so that Lance would see that the dog was taking advantage of the cool water. It was a hot summer day in southern California.

Lance had a huge smile on his face because he knew that this was one of many steps towards getting himself a dog.

They gathered up the bowl and food and treats and walked in a wider arc than necessary in order to make the dog not feel threatened. They sat the bowl with the food in it about a foot closer than it had been earlier in the day. Ray didn't think he was going to have to use the treats to attract the dog, but he had them just in case. They sat in the swing and Ray told Lance, "See the key to this is to make him think we aren't watching him, and we don't really care if he comes over here or not. We're just two guys hanging out in the park, sitting on the swings. We don't mind that there's a dog hanging around, we have no ulterior motives, we're just chilling."

“Right, just two guys.” Lance agreed.

“I think the more he gets used to you or us just being here, the more he’ll figure it’s not an issue.” Ray began. “I have a feeling that he probably belonged to somebody once, he doesn’t act like humans completely scare him, he just isn’t sure he can trust us yet.”

“Why would somebody get rid of him though?” Lance asked.

“Well, there could be reasons, some people just don’t take responsibility, and sometimes things happen.” Ray said. “I knew a family that moved, and their dog tried to go back to where they used to live. Maybe Lucky did that and his family couldn’t find him. Or maybe his owner got sick and couldn’t take care of him anymore so Lucky set out on his own to try to find food and shelter.”

“Well, I hope when he’s my dog he doesn’t decide to go back to his old family.” Lance said sadly.

“Oh, no, I’m sure he won’t. If he had a family or knew where to find them, he wouldn’t be hanging out here hoping to find scraps in Sally’s trash bins or for the scraps you’ve been bringing him. No, he’s either lost and can’t go home or something happened to his family, and he had to set out to take care of himself.”

By this time, Lucky had timidly walked over to the bowl of food he was on the furthest side from them, but he wasn’t hesitating to eat. He did keep his eyes up watching for any sudden movement, but he didn’t stop eating. When he had cleaned the bowl, Ray said “Here Lance, I’m going to give you one of the long sticks of jerky. You hold it out in your hand as far away from you as you can. When he starts sniffing at the air, smelling for it, slowly get out of the swing and keep it in front of you, take two steps, and kneel down and see if he’ll come take it from your hand. If he takes it, don’t move at all, see if he runs far away or if he only takes a few steps before starting to eat it”

Lance did the actions exactly as Ray had described them and the dog reacted the way Ray had said he would, he sniffed the air but stayed back until Lance was down on one knee holding the treat out as far as he could. Lucky tentatively approached the treat, sniffing the whole way. As soon as he could reach the treat with his neck stretched out, he bit into it with his teeth and took a few steps back, but he kept his eyes on Lance mostly, glancing at Ray only briefly a few times. When he realized that the boy wasn't going to attempt to catch him, he laid down and chewed on his jerky. He was out of arms reach from Lance, but not by a lot. If the boy took a step forward, he could touch the dog. It was obvious that the animal had been around humans before, and it also seemed to Ray like maybe he had a few humans that weren't always nice to him so he was hesitant as to who he could trust and how much he could trust them.

Lance remained still for the most part, but he did turn his head to give Ray a huge smile. He was feeling pretty confident that he was going to have a dog before long. But his smile faded a little at that thought. After the dog was done with its treat, he looked at Lance as if he were asking for another treat. This would be where the true test of his trust would come in. Both Ray and Lance would have to move in order for him to get another treat. Lance looked at the dog and said, "You want another treat, Lucky? I'll get you one, it's okay. Don't be scared." He turned toward Ray and reached out for another treat. Ray had to get partially out of his seat to be able to reach the boy.

"We're going to move slow, so he doesn't think we're doing anything to hurt him." Ray said. He pulled another stick out of the bag and stood up and took a step toward Lance so he could reach the treat. The dog was positioned to be ready to run if he felt the need, but the humans were moving slowly and carefully and not in his direction, so he felt safe and stayed waiting for another treat. Once Lance had the treat in his hand, Ray said, "This time, don't put your arm out as far, keep your elbow bent a little so that he has to come a little closer to you if he wants the treat."

Lance did that and the dog again came tentatively, but he still took the treat and didn't go far before sitting down to eat it. He wasn't ready to eat out of the boy's hand yet, but he wasn't nearly as afraid of Lance as he used to be.

Ray realized that it was getting late in the day, and close to dinner time. He wasn't really sure what to do with that though. Likely, he and Lance would both be eating at Sally's since that was the only place in town to get a meal, but the boy likely wouldn't want Ray to buy him another meal, so he had to make it seem like he wasn't worried about the boy eating or not. Of course, he was worried about it, but it had to seem like no pressure to Lance. "Well, I'm getting kind of hungry myself." he began. "I think Lucky's probably good for today. I think I'm going to head to Sally's to grab a bite."

Lance thought about that for a minute and finally said, "Yeah, I'll walk with you, if you want."

"Sure, that would be great." They both got up and Lucky took a few steps towards the woods, but he didn't run in fear, he just wanted to remain out of reach. As they walked along, Ray said, "That's probably the only bad thing about living in a small town, there's really only one place to eat. Not that Sally doesn't have good food, but you know, sometimes you want something different."

"Yeah, my dad used to take me to a place in the next town over that had really good pizza." Lance said, "I used to love going there. I haven't had pizza in forever."

"What do you like on your pizza?"

"Dad always got ham and bacon." Lance began, "with extra cheese. He made me try it with green peppers on it because he said those are good for you and I didn't mind that much."

Ray could tell that very likely it wouldn't have mattered what was on the pizza if the boy was sharing it with his dad. "Maybe we can go get some if your mom doesn't mind, or I can go grab one and bring it to the park sometime." Ray offered.

"Really, that would be awesome!" Lance said enthusiastically. They had reached Sally's and Lance hesitated to go inside. If he wasn't with Ray, he would walk in and find a job that needed to be done and do it to pay for his dinner.

Ray tried to put the boy's mind at ease by saying "I know your aunt may need you to help out, so if you can't sit with me, that's okay. I wouldn't want to interfere with you helping her. I'm sure she really appreciates everything you do for her."

"Yeah, I'm gonna see what she needs done." Lance said and walked into the diner.

Ray followed him in and took a seat in one of the booths near the door. Sally looked up and immediately spotted both of them, she walked over to Lance, and they had a conversation that Ray couldn't hear. The boy walked over to the closet and grabbed out the broom and dust pan while Sally headed in his direction.

“You didn’t need to pay for Lance’s lunch.” Sally said, she sounded a little upset by his actions.

“I know, but he and I had a deal that I was buying him lunch. I know that you don’t require him to do work here to get his meals, but he does it anyway because that’s what he was taught. I don’t want him to think that he’s not working for his food if that’s what makes it okay for him. He showed me the northeast section of town today and introduced me to several people. I consider it money well spent to buy him lunch for showing me around and acquainting me with some of the people.”

Sally acknowledged that he had a point.

“I suspect we will be doing the same the next three days.” Ray stated. “I did wonder though; he mentioned some pizza place that his dad used to take him to. Without having met his mom, and not really wanting to interfere on her grief or whatever is going on, I don’t want to take Lance in my car, but I was wondering if you might know what pizza place, he is talking about and maybe I could pick some up sometime.”

“Yeah, that would be G’s pizza, best pizza around these parts. It’s about ten miles up the road.” Sally said.

“I know you are Lance’s aunt, but where are you connected?” Ray asked.

“My husband and his daddy were brothers.” Sally stated.

“I know it’s none of my business, but does his mom at least take care of him?” Ray asked. “Lance has only told me enough for me to know that she must be suffering from a lot of grief or something.”

“He has a roof over his head, he gets his meals here if he needs them.” Sally stated defensively. “Everyone in town watches out for him. I need to keep moving, do you know what you want?”

Ray didn’t have to have it spelled out to him any more clearly, Sally wasn’t going to share anything more about the situation. “Yeah, I’ll have a bacon cheeseburger with a side of fries and a root beer.”

Shortly after Sally walked away, Lance put the broom away and came and sat in the booth with Ray. Sally brought out their plates and Lance too had gotten a cheeseburger, but without the bacon.

"So, what part of town do you want to show me tomorrow, or would you rather take a day off?" Ray asked.

"Well, we can meet at the school like you said, and shoot some hoops maybe." Lance began.

"Oh, yeah, for sure, between breakfast and lunch we'll play." Ray agreed. "And we have to make sure Lucky gets fed, but maybe after lunch you can show me another part of town. Maybe where you live."

"Maybe." Lance said softly.

"Or not, it can be another part too."

"It's just that my mom doesn't really like to have people come over if she doesn't know that they're going to be there." Lance explained.

"Oh, yeah, for sure." Ray agreed. "A lot of people are like that. I didn't mean we have to go in, I'd just like to see where you live. You think about it and decide tomorrow which way we're going to head out after lunch."

"Okay." Lance agreed.

Ray needed to change the subject, so he said "I think Lucky is starting to get used to you a little. He didn't run as far away to eat the treats as he used to."

"I noticed that." Lance sounded much happier with this subject. "I hope it means he'll be my dog soon."

"Well, I don't know if it will be super soon, but I'm pretty sure it will happen." Ray insisted.

They didn't really talk about anything in particular for the rest of the meal and then they parted ways. Ray went to pick up his SUV and Lance headed home, wherever that was.

The rest of the week, they maintained the same basic schedule, they met, they played basketball or catch, they had lunch and they explored the town.

Their second day of exploration, Lance showed Ray the northwest section of town. He pointed out another church, and two more homes that belonged to his friends. Ray was glad that Lance seemed to have a good group of friends, even if they were all away right now. The death of his father and whatever was going on with his mother didn't seem to have made him withdraw from friendships with his peers.

They passed a small doctor's office that had a sign saying they also provided prompt care services. That was a new concept to Ray. In LA, there were doctors and there were hospitals and there were places that were designated as urgent care. Ray supposed in a small town, you had to adjust accordingly and sometimes be both. "Do you have a hospital here?" he asked.

"No, but there's one not too far from here." Lance said.

"That's good then." Ray said.

Lance pointed out his Aunt Sally's house. It was a nice looking two story home. He had also pointed out a couple of small boutique type shops. Ray would try to find time to stop in to the shops someday. He was sure Lance wasn't interested, but it had always fascinated Ray to see what types of unique things one could find in such a shop.

They finished their day at Sally's. Ray told Sally he would wait a bit to order, Lance was busy wrapping silverware in napkins and would eat when he was done. Ray just asked for coffee until Lance was ready to eat. He would spend as much time as he could helping the boy feel like he wasn't alone in the world.

Their third day of exploration was in the southeast section of town. It was more of what he had seen on the other two days, several houses, a few shops, another church. By the end of the day, Ray wasn't sure if Lance's house was in the one remaining section, or if he had chosen not to go down the street it was on. They had been going up and down various streets where Lance had wanted to show him something, but they hadn't gone on every street in town. Tomorrow would be the deciding factor on whether or not Lance was trying to keep Ray from knowing where he lived.

On the fourth day, Lance showed Ray the last of the three churches he had said were in town. When they got to the end of a block, Lance pointed and said, “That house down there, the third one, that’s my house.” He didn’t start down the street, so Ray didn’t push for a closer look. From this distance, it didn’t look like the house was in any ill repair, the lawn looked like it could use a good mowing, but that wasn’t uncommon for a single mother. Especially if they didn’t own a lawn mower. Now that he knew where it was, he planned to drive by on occasion, just to check on the place. They finished their way back around to the park. It was Friday, so as promised, Ray went to get the pizza.

# Chapter 4

When Ray got back with the pizza, they ate it in the park. Lucky wasn't far away hoping for a scrap or two and they obliged him with pieces of their crust. They had given him his dog food and turned on the water faucet first, so they figured it wouldn't be a bad thing to give him a little human food.

On Saturday, the entire town seemed to be out in full force to celebrate Founder's Day. Lance had promised Ray that he was going to try to get his mom to come to the picnic so that they could meet. Ray had told him to do his best, but if she didn't want to come, that would be okay. He didn't want the boy feeling like a failure or like he had let his friend down if whatever was going on with the mom made her not willing to come.

When Ray saw Lance walking toward the crowd with a young woman, he couldn't help the thoughts that went through his head. One, she was a beautiful woman in theory, but she looked almost haunted. Ray couldn't fully see her face, the distance was too far for that, but her face definitely didn't have a smile. Her hair was combed, but it looked like she may not have had it cut or trimmed in a while. The other thing that stood out to Ray was that it was close to a hundred degrees out, and she was wearing a long sleeved shirt. He hoped that didn't mean what he feared it meant. He had been around enough people in LA to get a sense of just what was probably going on. He approached Lance and his mom slowly.

He cheerfully said, "Hey Lance, is this your mom?"

Lance looked excited for the two pieces of his world to meet, he said, "Mom, this is my friend Ray, the one I've been hanging out with this week. Ray, this is my mom, her name is Hope."

Ray put out his hand and said, “It’s a pleasure to meet you.”

The woman shook it but didn’t meet his eye and said, “Nice to meet you too. Lance has been talking about you all week.”

Ray wished he could say the same. He was pretty sure that the problem that was keeping Hope from participating more fully in her son’s life wasn’t about the grief, but the way she was dealing with that grief. She hadn’t looked him directly in the eye, but he was still pretty sure that her pupils would be dilated, and her eyes would be droopy. He could also tell that her clothes were too big for her, most likely she had lost weight, although that could be caused by either grief or drug abuse so that wasn’t necessarily a sure tell. He would try to observe, and now that he had a better idea of what to ask, he would talk to Sally and maybe even Maude. He didn’t want to condemn the woman, just the opposite, he wanted to get her help if she would let him. But he knew from past experience confronting her head on when he was basically a stranger wouldn’t likely do much good.

“I was hoping to ask you a question, if I may.” Ray began. “I was wondering if you would be okay with me giving Lance rides in my SUV. I haven’t wanted to take him anywhere until I asked you and I wouldn’t take him anywhere outside of town other than maybe to the pizza place or a McDonald’s or something. I assure you, I’m a safe driver and I think Maude and Sally would vouch for the fact that I’m a decent guy.”

Maude must have heard her name because she turned and said “Oh, yes, Ray has been staying at my place all week. He’s a very nice man. We sit and talk in the evenings over a cup of tea. You can trust him with Lance.”

“Well, I’m sure a trip for pizza or McDonald’s would be fine, but mostly just around town.” She stated.

“Yay!” Lance yelled. “He got pizza and brought it to the park, but it’s not the same as being able to go there and get it.”

“Well, just let me or Aunt Sally know if you’re going out of town, so we don’t worry.” Hope said.

“Okay,” Lance said. “I’m going to go get food.” He started to race off, but before he could get far, Ray had put a hand out to stop him.

“Lance, that’s not how you should talk to your mother.” Ray said.

Lance stopped and turned to his mom and said, “Sorry, can I go eat?”

“Sure.” Hope said softly.

“Would you like to grab a plate; I’d love to have a chance to talk to you. Lance hasn’t really told me much about you.” Ray said.

“Actually, I’m not feeling all that well.” she said. “I think I should go home. Please tell Lance he knows what time he has to be home by.” She turned and walked back the way she came.

Ray felt like he had made a big mistake, but Maude was right there to assure him. “Don’t take it personally, she hasn’t been seen out in public since her husband died except to grocery shop and even that doesn’t happen often. I would imagine she only came out today to see who Lance has been jabbering on about. “

“She’s basically become a hermit.” Sally said as she walked up to them.

“Well, does anyone know why, I mean I know her husband died, but you guys are family, and this is a close knit community, I would think someone has reached out.” Ray said.

“Oh, we’ve done plenty of reaching out, but she isn’t interested.” Maude said.

Ray didn’t want to get into all of this with Maude present, because she wasn’t family to Hope and Lance. But he was definitely planning to try to get a chance to talk to Sally alone sometime to see if his suspicions were right. If they were, he was hoping they could come up with a plan to help the young woman so that Lance could have a better home life.

He went to find Lance and grab some food. Thanks to his tours, Ray felt like he already knew several of the people in town. The ones he hadn’t met before had apparently heard of him and had a general idea of who he was. It was a friendly town. He hoped that maybe he could get them to band together to help one of their own.

He enjoyed the afternoon and getting to know more people. If it weren't for his wanderlust, this would be a great town to live in and he had a feeling he would visit again someday. When he found himself near Sally, he asked, "Is there a time that maybe you and I could sit and chat?"

"We close the diner at eight most nights, if you're there at closing time, I can sit for a few minutes." she said.

Ray got the feeling that the chat may not go well, or that Sally just wasn't interested in helping Hope, which made no sense to him, but maybe there had been bad blood between them or something in the past that had caused the relationship to sever. Maybe she had tried to help Hope before but hadn't been successful and thought it was a lost cause. Whatever the reason, he wouldn't find it out until the next day since the diner had closed for the picnic and fireworks that were to take place later.

As the sun started going down, the townsfolk made their way to the large field where the fireworks would be able to be seen, Ray looked around and didn't see Lance anywhere at first, which was puzzling because what little kid didn't like fireworks. Unless there was a noise issue, most loved them. He asked a man that was standing near the edge of the field if he had seen Lance at all and the man said, "Yeah, last I saw him he was headed up the street in that direction." He pointed towards the north end of town.

At first, that made no sense to Ray, if he had decided to go home, he would have headed the opposite way. Why would Lance go in that direction? And then it dawned on him, the park. Lance was heading toward the park, most likely to check on Lucky.

Ray ran towards the park but slowed as he got close enough to see what was going on. There were streetlights in the park so he could see the boy sitting near the edge of the woods with Lucky about ten feet away. He was talking softly, he looked up when he saw Ray but put a finger over his lips to warn Ray to be quiet. He nodded and stepped slowly closer so that he could hear the boy, he remained far enough away that the dog wasn't really paying attention to him.

"Hey Lucky," the boy said. "In a few minutes, they're going to start making a whole bunch of noise down there, and I want you to know that it's nothing for you to be afraid of. I'm right here if you need someone to help you not be afraid. I won't let anything hurt you."

The dog had its ears perked up listening to the boy, but as of yet wasn't making any effort to either get closer or to run away. Ray crouched down to watch and offer suggestions if it were needed or consolation if the dog rejected Lance's comfort.

The first boom came from somewhere behind Ray, and the dog's ears perked up. It stood up as if it were ready to run, but Lance very calmly said "It's okay boy, it's not going to hurt you, I won't let it." He held out his hand toward the dog, he kept it low so there was no way it could be considered a threat. The dog sniffed tentatively in the air. He was hoping for food, but would he be willing to take comfort or protection? Another loud boom sounded and again the dog looked toward town, looked at Lance, looked at the woods behind him and contemplated running. But Lance remained steadfast, holding out his hand to offer whatever the dog would take from him, speaking softly encouraging the dog to accept his help.

Ray wouldn't have believed it if he hadn't seen it, because he had been sure that the dog's trust was a way off yet, but he stepped into Lance's hand and lowered his head so that Lance could rub his ear. Lance encouraged him "See, boy, I'm not going to hurt you. I want to be your friend." Another loud boom sounded, and the dog thrust its body into Lance's. Lance cradled the dog's head to him, doing his best to cover both ears. He didn't force the dog to be held tightly, but with each boom and each shriek of the fireworks, the dog buried its head deeper and deeper into Lances comforting arms. Ray was pretty sure that the dog had belonged to someone in the past and likely had faced some abuse of some kind. At least Ray would guess that was the reason for it being so scared of the loud noises. There may be other reasons though. Either way, he was happy to see that the dog had realized that Lance wouldn't hurt it and it could accept comfort from the boy.

Lance looked up at Ray with eyes as big as saucers and a smile that practically glowed. Ray remained quiet, the dog had accepted Lance, it may not be fully sure about him yet, but it definitely saw Lance as a protector rather than a threat. Ray gave him a thumbs up but otherwise didn't move.

When the fireworks had ended, the dog waited several more minutes to be sure that it was over, the grand finale at the end had made the dog cower even more and shake in fear even though Lance was holding him tightly. When he finally felt confident that the noise wasn't going to continue, he pulled away a little and Lance let him. The boy realized that forcing him to stay wasn't going to help with the progress of the relationship. The dog gave

Lance's cheek one lick as if the dog were thanking him for his kindness and support and then he trotted away back to the edge of the woods.

"Did you see that?" Lance exclaimed.

"I did, he's trusting you more all the time, he trusts you to keep him safe." Ray said, "That's a huge step forward. I have a feeling that he's had someone treat him unkindly in the past, so he isn't going to go all in easily, but you have made a lot of progress. He's still not completely sure about you, and he's definitely not sure about me, but he's starting to learn trust. If he was abused or mistreated, that isn't going to come easy for him and it may be on a case by case basis for a while."

"What do you mean?" Lance asked.

"Well, like tonight, he came to you for comfort and protection, but then moved away when he thought the threat was gone." Ray said. "He's not one hundred percent in, but if he knows he can trust you for protection, it won't be long before he's sure you're okay. That's why I think maybe someone was mean to him. He trusted them and then all of a sudden he couldn't trust them, and it was confusing for him because they changed."

"Why would someone do that though?" Lance asked.

"Oh, you never know. Sometimes people are having a bad day, sometimes they're sick or something." Ray said. He was kind of thinking of Hope and her situation. "Like with your mom, not that she would be mean to a dog, I'm not saying that. But she's a different person now than she was before your dad died, right?"

"Yeah." Lance said somberly.

"So, something like that." Ray suggested. "Maybe they had him and then got sick or had a death in the family or something and they didn't intend to be mean to him, but they just had so much going on."

"Maybe." Lance said. "I hope he figures out that I would never hurt him."

"I'm sure he will, just give him time." Ray said. "It's getting pretty late, we better head back into town and get you home before your mom worries about you."

Lance stood up, took one more look back towards the woods where Lucky had gone and then joined Ray at the sidewalk and headed toward town.

“You know, another thing that I just thought about with Lucky, is that part of the reason he is so scared is that people who don’t know his situation might have been harsh with him and he’s just not sure anymore.” Ray said.

“What do you mean? How were they harsh?” Lance asked.

“Well, I’m not saying she did, I’m just using this as a comparison, okay?” Ray asked. At Lance’s nod, he continued. “Someone like your Aunt Sally. She said Lucky had been getting into her trash, maybe he did that with other people too and maybe one of them was super mean or scary and it made him not sure who to trust. Does that make sense?”

“Yeah.” Lance agreed. “Like they just meant to get him out of their trash, but they did it in a way that made them seem like they were going to hurt him or something like that.”

“Right, they may not even have realized that they were being like that.” Ray said. “They wanted to scare him out of the trash, but they weren’t intending to hurt him.”

“Sometimes people misunderstand too.” Lance said.

“Yes, they do Lance.’ Ray agreed, “Yes, they do.”

# Chapter 5

The following day, Lance and Ray were both at the diner for breakfast. It was Sunday and though Maude had offered to make a breakfast before she went to church, Ray had told her he was fine with going to the diner so she could have a day of rest.

Ray told Lance, "I think I'm going up to Joshua Tree today to take a few pictures, I've been here for a week and haven't done that yet. That will give you a chance to see if Lucky is more comfortable with you when I'm not around. But I'll be back by four this afternoon so that we can go get dinner. We can do pizza or McDonald's, whichever you pick. I'm going to give you a bag with some food and the bowl and treats and stuff so that you can make sure Lucky gets fed this morning and I'll be back in time to make sure he gets more for tonight, okay?"

"Okay." Lance didn't seem overjoyed by the idea, but he wasn't going to complain about a day alone if he was going to get to go out for dinner later.

Ray made sure to tell Sally that he and Lance wouldn't be there for dinner, but he would stop by closer to closing time to grab a slice of pie and have a chat. Sally didn't look overly cheerful about that, but she knew it was inevitable.

Ray headed up to the national park, before he got out of his car, he decided to try to call Maude's son. Sally had given him the number. When the man answered, Ray said, "You don't know me, but I got your number from Sally at the diner in Thousand Palms. I've been renting a room from your mom for a week or so now."

“Is my mom, okay?” the man asked immediately.

“She is, she’s fine, well other than really missing her kids and grandkids.” Ray stated.

“Yeah, I know, it’s just so hard to get time off and it’s really far away.” Bill jr. said.

“Well, I have a thought that might help with that, if you think you and your siblings would be interested.”

“What’s that?” he asked.

“Well, Maude had been so kind to me that I would like to buy her a simple tablet and help her get it set up with video calling. I’m told that for no more than she would be using, the bill would only be about ten dollars a month for the Internet. Would you and your siblings be able to connect with her that way. We could agree on an app that you think would work best for all of you.” Ray explained. “I thought about getting a cell phone, but I think that Maude would find that a burden because she would feel like she had to carry it around all the time. That’s why I was thinking a tablet might be best. It could sit on her table or counter, and you could still use the landline to call her to set up times for a video call.”

“Wow, that would be amazing.” Maude’s son said. “I’m sure my brother and sister would be happy to have that opportunity too. We’ve all tried to get mom to move closer, but that house had too many memories for her. That’s where she and my dad raised us. But it would be great to be able to do that.”

“Well, I’m a photographer of sorts, and she asked me to take a picture to send to her grandkids so they wouldn’t forget what she looks like.” Ray stated. “This idea just came to me as possibly a better option.”

“Oh, man, it’s an awesome idea. I for sure will let my siblings know and we’ll be set up whenever you have it ready on your end. Just let us know what program you decide on.” the young man said.

“Sounds good.” Ray agreed, I’ll be in touch then.”

Ray hung up the phone and got his camera equipment out of the trunk of the car. He spent the day wandering around the national park and taking photos, some he just wanted for his personal memories and some that might be sellable to a magazine or other publication. It was a beautiful place, but he could pretty much see it all in under a day. He would send the files of the photos to some of his friends and see if any of them wanted anything more specific taken, otherwise he probably wouldn't need to come back. Which meant that he didn't need to stay in Thousand Palms for his photography pursuits, but he was going to stay a little while longer to see if he could help Lance and his mom, and it would take a few days at least to get Maude's tablet and help her get used to how to use it.

Ray was back at the small town park by three thirty that afternoon. Lance was sitting on the ground with Lucky a few feet away, they both looked like they were just hanging out although the dog still maintained a bit of space.

When Lance saw Ray arrive, he spoke to the dog and told him "See, boy. I told you Ray would be back and he's brought more food for you, I'm sure." He turned to Ray and smiled and said, "He let me pet him a little, after I fed him this morning. After I came back from lunch, he's just stayed over there, but he listens to me talk."

Oh, what Ray wouldn't give to have heard the things the boy said to that dog. He was sure that Lance had felt he could open up and be honest and say things to the dog that he couldn't say to other humans. The dog was quickly becoming his best friend and would hear all of his stories, would know all of his fears and would keep all his secrets.

"Sounds like you two had a good day hanging out." Ray said. He got more food out of the back of his SUV and walked towards the pair. He approached slowly and stayed on the other side of Lance so the dog would feel that he had his protector guarding him. He opened the can, and handed it to Lance, the bowl was laying on the ground not far away, so the boy could easily fill it without having to make large or sudden movements that might startle the dog.

When the bowl was full Lance pushed it a few feet closer to Lucky and then sat back. "Did you take lots of pictures at the place?"

"I did." Ray said. "I kind of made a deal with some friends of mine back in Los Angeles that I would take pictures of places like that and send them back and they would maybe send me money if they liked them, so I had to go get that taken care of. But that's done so for however much longer I stay here, I shouldn't have to go away again. If they see a part they want better pictures of or more closeup or whatever they'll let me know and I might have to go for a few hours to get the specific ones they want. But other than that, I'm finished with it."

"I wish you could stay here forever." Lance said.

"I know, I'd like that too," Ray agreed. "But I will have to move on eventually, it's just a part of life. But I am staying here for a while longer and I'll definitely stay until things are settled with you and Lucky. That way you'll have a friend to hang out with when I have to be gone."

"Yeah, that will be good." Lance said somberly.

"Is something else going on?" Ray asked.

"No, it's just that my mom isn't always great at remembering to take care of me, that's why I go do work for Aunt Sally, I don't know if she's going to be okay with helping me take care of Lucky." he explained.

"Well, we'll take that on when we get there." Ray said. He wasn't going to make any promises to Lance, but if he had his way about things, there would be lots of changes coming up. Lance would have a full family to take care of both he and Lucky. Actually, he was going to do whatever it took to make sure the boy was taken care of. He hoped it would go in a positive way and Lance's mom would get help, if not, he was prepared to have it go the not so great way and make sure Lance was protected. He definitely didn't want Lance growing up and starting to use drugs to help ease his pain from not having either parent being an active part of his life anymore.

While Lucky was eating the food, Ray got up and went to turn the faucet on. Someone had turned it off at some point, and that was expected, but he wanted to make sure the dog got good clean drinking water as much as he could. It hadn't really rained since he had gotten here a week ago, a few sprinkles, but not enough to make sure that any standing water that Lucky might find wouldn't be stagnant.

When the dog had emptied his dish and meandered over to the faucet to lap up some water, Ray asked, "So, McDonald's or pizza?"

"McDonald's, we had pizza last week and even though it's better when we have it there instead of here, I haven't been to McDonald's in forever."

Lance said.

Ray knew how he would finish that sentence if his brain would let him. He hadn't been there since the last time his dad had been able to take him and his mom, most likely on one of his trips home on leave. "McDonald's it is then. Maybe we can do pizza some other time."

Lance jumped up and grabbed the food bowl. They had agreed that they wouldn't leave it in the park. It would always stay with one of them because they didn't know if Lucky would drag it off or if someone would see it and think it was left behind by someone and think it was trash. As he walked to the car, he looked toward the dog and said, "I'll be back later, boy. I'll try and bring you a hamburger." He looked towards Ray and added, "Maybe."

Ray took the dish from Lance and asked, "Why did you add, maybe to that sentence?"

"Well, you're already buying me food, I didn't know if you would want to buy extra, and you told me that we shouldn't let Lucky get used to eating human food too much, so he stays out of Aunt Sally's garbage, so I wasn't sure." Lance explained.

"Well, that second part is true for sure, but I think he is learning to count on you to keep him fed more than he is worried about what kind of food you're feeding him. So, it's not as big of a deal if he gets a bit of human food from you now and then. It's more about him not thinking he has to find it on his own." Ray stated. "As to the other part, I don't mind you asking me for things, Lance. We're friends. Now that doesn't mean that I'm going to buy you everything you ever want but buying a hamburger for Lucky isn't a big request." He wouldn't say anything about the fact that he had already made up his mind that he was willing to do a lot for this boy. If he could work out the plan that was forming in his head, he would be putting a lot of time and possibly money into helping the boy have a better life. They got into the SUV and he told Lance to buckle up. He pulled out of the park and headed towards the fast food place. "So, I was thinking, maybe while I'm here, we can see if your mom or your Aunt Sally are willing to help us catch up on your schoolwork."

"I don't think they will. My mom's sick and Aunt Sally has so much to do already." Lance said. "Besides, Uncle Steve doesn't like having me around a lot."

That was the first time that Ray had even heard the man's name, he knew he existed of course, but he was always back in the kitchen cooking whenever Ray had been to the restaurant. "Why doesn't he like having you around?"

"I don't know, he used to come over all the time when my dad would come home, but since then, he doesn't really like me I think." Lance said sadly.

"Well, maybe it's just hard for him if he used to hang out with your dad a lot." Ray guessed.

"Maybe."

That gave Ray pause, if the uncle had a reason to not like Lance, would he be willing to help in the plan Ray was working on? They didn't talk the rest of the way, it wasn't really that long of a drive anyway, but they both most likely had things on their mind.

When they got there though, Lance was back to being an enthusiastic young boy again. Ray let him order anything he wanted including a chocolate shake and a hot fudge sundae. Normally Ray wouldn't let a kid eat that much sweet stuff, but he had done a good job with his actual protein and it wasn't like anything at McDonald's was overly healthy.

They had ordered two plain cheeseburgers to take back to Lucky. Ray figured that the boy would be anxious to take them to the park and that would give him some time to sit down and talk to Sally and get her thoughts on the entire situation with Lance and his mother and apparently his uncle. He was really hoping that he could get both Sally and her husband on board with his plan. But that would remain to be seen. He pulled up in front of Sally's and parked. "I promised Sally that I'd stop in just before closing for a slice of pie or something. Do you want to go in, or are you in a hurry to get to the park?"

"I think I should get these to Lucky and make sure the water is still on since it's almost night time and I don't know if he has a place to get water at night." Lance said.

"That's good thinking. You're going to make a great dog owner. It means a lot to an animal when you think so much about it." Ray praised. "So, I have some business to discuss with Sally after she closes, so I may not be done for a while. I'll swing by the park and see if you are still there, but don't stay out too late waiting for me if I'm not there, okay?"

"Okay." Lance agreed. "I'll see you tomorrow, right?"

"Definitely, I'll be bringing Lucky's food over after I eat with Maude." Ray assured.

"See you in the morning." Lance said and he raced off to feed his dog.

Ray stepped into the diner and Sally looked up when she heard the door chime. It was mostly quiet in the diner, just one couple finishing up their food. Ray went and sat in the booth in the far back corner so that he wouldn't be seen by the window into the kitchen. He didn't know if Sally would be more comfortable talking to him without her husband watching or not. But he was going to give her as much leeway as he possibly could. He couldn't imagine that there would be anything that would keep her from wanting to help Lance but wanting to and being able to were very different things for some people. If her husband was controlling or abusive or somehow overbearing and had told her she could only go so far when it came to helping Lance, then he would have to go another route, it was one he really didn't want to have to go, but if it was the only way to get Lance in a healthy situation, he might have to do things that didn't really appeal to him.

Sally asked him what kind of pie he wanted, and she brought him over a slice of banana cream. "I'll lock up as soon as the Anderson's leave and be back to have out chat."

Ray ate his pie and tried to get his thoughts together. He couldn't imagine anyone not wanting to help Lance and his mom, especially family, but sometimes things happened to cause distance. He knew that from experience. His father had left his mom years ago and had moved away and had another family. Ray hadn't met his half-brother, he had never wanted to. But as he had gotten older, he had wondered what the man would be like. He knew where the man lived, maybe on his trip around the country, he would try to find him. He would have to give that some more thought.

When Sally came and sat in the booth with him she had brought them each a cup of coffee.

"So, I want to know how to help Lance and in order to do that, I need to know exactly what's going on. It seems like your husband isn't on board with doing anything to help the situation." Ray stated. "Why do I get that impression?"

"Well," she hesitated and took a deep breath and let it out slowly. "It's not that he doesn't want to help, it's that it's difficult for him to be around Lance."

"In what way?" Ray asked puzzled.

"Just a minute." Sally got up and went behind the counter and came back with what looked like a piece of paper at first. When she got closer, Ray could tell it was a photograph. She passed it to him across the table.

"Yeah, this is a picture of Lance, what's that got to do with it?" he asked.

"No, that's a picture of Lance's daddy. My husband's brother." Sally explained, "It's not that he doesn't want to help with Lance, it's that it hurts so much every time he looks at that little boy."

Ray paused for a minute, he could understand the man's pain, but it didn't change the fact that Lance needed people he could rely on. "So, he's not willing to help at all?"

"NO!" Sally said, "It's not that at all, but we have tried to talk to Hope. She doesn't want help, and other than bringing in law enforcement, we don't know what to do. That's why we always have food for Lance. I know he won't just come in and eat, his daddy taught him not to take a handout, so we let him do things so he feels like he's paying his own way."

"I know you don't want to get law enforcement involved, but there may be some things that can be done that still protects Lance and gets help for his mom." Ray offered.

"Like what?" Sally asked.

"I have a friend whose wife works with CPS in Los Angeles." Ray began, "I'm going to ask some questions without giving any names, but I need to know what your level of commitment is before I call him."

“What do you mean?” she asked.

“Well, I would like to ask if he can be kept out of the system if there’s a family member that is willing to step in and become his guardian for however long it takes for Hope to get clean.” Ray said.

Sally had her face turned down and was thinking about how to answer that, when a voice spoke up from behind the counter of the diner. “We’ll take him if you can make it so that she doesn’t go to jail. I don’t want that for her, but I do want that boy to have a chance in life.”

Ray assumed the man was Sally’s husband, he had a strong family resemblance to Lance. “That’s what I am hoping for, but at some point, Hope has to be willing to go to rehab or something like it because us wanting to keep law enforcement out of it doesn’t go very far if she’s getting drugs from a dealer. If she ever gets caught buying, it could be all over for her.”

“You call your friend and see if we can get the guardianship part, and then we’ll see if we can work together to get Hope some help.” Sally said.

“That’s great, thank you so much.” Ray said, “On another note, Lance tells me that he’s going to be held back in school if he can’t do some make-up work this summer. I’d be glad to help with some of it if I can, but I don’t think his teacher is just going to hand me the information I need. With all the privacy laws, I may not be able to get far.”

“I’ll call Vickie and see what we can do to get the work all put together.” Sally said. “That’s his teacher from last year, she and I went to school together, so I’m pretty sure I can get her to help us get what’s needed.”

“Sounds like a plan,” Ray said standing up. “I’ll call my friend tomorrow, although it may take a day or two for him to run it past his wife and get back to me.” He walked over to the counter where the man stood and held out his hand. When the man took it, he said, “I’m very sorry for your loss, but for what it’s worth, I think it would mean a lot to your brother that you’ve agreed to help Lance.”

“I know.” Steve said. “It’s really hard to see that boy’s face, but I can’t let that stop me from making sure he has a better life.”

Ray made his way back to Maude's and as usual, she was in front of her television watching a game show. He sat in the chair beside hers and asked, "How was your day, Maude?"

"It was as good as any other, I suppose." she said.

"Well, I think I can make it a good day." Ray stated.

Maude turned off the TV and said "Oh, how's that?"

"Why don't we go have our cup of tea, and I'll tell you." Ray said. He was actually going to miss having a cup of chamomile tea with Maude every evening when it was time for him to move on.

Maude went to the kitchen and began preparing the tea. When she brought it and two cups to the table, Ray began, "I know you said you wanted me to take your picture so that your grandkids won't forget what you look like, but I think I have an even better idea."

"And what would that be?" she asked skeptically.

"I would like to buy you a tablet, it's kind of like a cellphone, but you wouldn't have to worry about taking it places like a phone because it's not for calls. We can download a program that makes it so that you can do a video call with any of your kids or grandkids."

"I'd be able to see them and talk to them?" she asked.

"Yep, I called your son today, and he's totally on board with that plan and he said he'll make sure the others know about it too." Ray said cheerfully. "Once the tablet arrives, I'll call him again and we'll agree to what program everyone thinks is best and I'll help you learn how to use it."

Maude had tears in her eyes when she said "Oh, Ray, I don't even know what to say. That would mean so much to me. For however much longer you're here, you stay for free. I won't take another cent from you. Do you need the rent that you've already paid back to get this tablet thing?"

"Oh, no, Maude, they aren't that expensive really." Ray began. "But you will have to get Internet here, Sally tells me that will cost you about ten dollars a month. She can help us get it figured out for who we have to call or whatever to get it set up for you."

"You are truly a godsend, Ray, you truly are." Maude praised.

"Well, I do have a bit of a favor to ask in return." Ray said.

"Anything, you name it." she offered.

"Well, I'm hoping that I can help Lance catch up on some schoolwork and I don't really have a place to do that. We could try the diner, but I'm afraid that would be distracting with the bell and the people. The park isn't really a good idea either, with possible people and that stray dog he's determined to win over. I was hoping maybe you would be okay with me helping him here at your kitchen table sometimes." Ray said.

"Oh, yes, that's fine." Maude said with a smile, "My children studied here many a night. It will be nice to have someone here. Maybe I can bake some cookies or cakes or things that he can have as a treat when he does well on his studies."

"I am sure he would consider that an awesome incentive." Ray said.

They finished their tea, just chatting about things in town and the photos Ray had taken at the national park. He pulled up some of them on the tablet he had uploaded the memory card to and showed her a few of them.

"It's been years since I've been there." Maude said. "But it's still just as pretty."

"Well, if you ever want to go back, I'd be glad to take you while I'm here." Ray offered.

"I'll think about that." she said. "I'm going to call it a night, although I'm not sure I'll fall asleep easy, I will be thinking about the day when I get to see my grandbabies faces again."

"It shouldn't take too many days." Ray said.

"Well, goodnight, Ray, and thank you again." With that, she walked down the short hallway that led to the master bedroom and Ray made his way up the stairs. He scrolled through the photos again and realized that he needed to take photos here in Thousand Palms of all the people who were becoming friends that he never wanted to forget. He sent the file to his friend and told him that if any of them were useable for the magazine to let him know. He also told him he wasn't moving on for a while so if there was something they liked but wanted different angles of he could go back.

# Chapter 6

The following morning, Ray enjoyed his breakfast with Maude and then made his way to the park to find Lance. The boy was sitting at a picnic table and the dog wasn't too far off although it alerted and took a few steps further away when it saw Ray approaching. It didn't go far though because he could see that Ray had the dish and the food with him. He got the food into the dish and then had Lance set it on the ground a few feet away. He hoped the dog would feel safe around him, but it was imperative that the dog associated Lance with being fed. Ray didn't need the dog's loyalty, Lance did. Especially if the plan Ray was setting in motion came to fruition.

They waited until the dog was finished with his food to turn on the water faucet and when the dog went to get his drink, Ray began one of the many conversations he would be needing to have with Lance. "So, I was talking to your Aunt Sally, and I told her about the schoolwork that needs to be done. She's going to talk to your teacher and let her know that I'm willing to help you. Maude said we could use her kitchen table as a study place, and she even said something about maybe baking some cookies so we can have a reward when we get an assignment done or whatever. How does that sound?"

"It sounds okay. I don't really want to have to do the work but doing it with you will be good. And that will make it so I can go to the next grade with my friends, right?" Lance asked.

"It should, if we can stay focused and get it all done." Ray encouraged. "We can go down to the diner and see if Sally has had a chance to contact your teacher yet if you want."

"Okay." Lance didn't sound overly enthused, but he did sound resolved to getting this taken care of if it meant that he could be with his friends instead of being held back. He picked up the dog dish and walked toward Ray's SUV.

When they got to the diner, Ray asked Sally if she had a chance to talk to the teacher yet. She responded, "Yep, she said if you two stop by, she'll give you the things that need to be done. Lance knows where her house is."

Lance gave him directions and when they got there, the teacher invited them both in. "I don't know if you want to take all of it at once, or if you want to focus on one subject at a time." She said, "I can do it either way."

"Why don't we start with one subject at time." Ray said. "Maybe I can call you or have Sally call you to let you know when we're getting close to needing more."

"I'd be glad to give you my number." the young woman said. "Feel free to call me if you ever have any questions about the directions or whatever. And if you get stuck on something, we can meet, and I can show you how to get through."

Ray had Lance take the book and the stack of assignments for the first subject out to the car while he got the teacher's number. "Thank you for letting me help him get this done, I know it means a lot to him to get to move ahead with his friends."

"Well, thank you for taking an interest in helping him." she said. "I know he has a rough home life, I'm glad he has an aunt and a friend that want to help him."

"Well, I'm trying to do everything I can to help his situation in a lot of ways." Ray stated. "Again, thank you for helping me help him." He walked to his SUV and drove to Sally's.

"Are we gonna have lunch before we get started?" Lance asked.

"We are, and today, I'm buying." Ray said. "I want us to get started on the schoolwork, so you don't have time to work for Sally, okay?"

"Okay." Lance agreed that boy was one hundred percent committed to whatever he set his mind to.

"Hey, Sally." Ray said as they walked in, "I'm buying Lance here lunch because when we leave, I'm going to put his brain to work studying hard for a while." He winked and he knew that Sally totally got the hint.

"Well, sounds like he'll be earning his lunch then." Sally said. "Do you know what you want, or do you need menus? The special today is sloppy joes and potato chips."

Ray looked at Lance and shrugged "Sounds pretty good to me, what do you think Lance?"

"Yeah, I'll have the special." Lance said. "And chocolate milk."

"I'll take coffee with mine." Ray said. When Sally walked away, he looked at Lance and said, "Your teacher started us with math. Is that one of your strong subjects or one of the weaker ones?"

"Oh, I like math." Lance said. "It's my favorite. "

"That's good then, this should be easy." Ray had no doubt that the teacher had done that on purpose. If she started him with subjects he liked and that would come easy to him, he would make quick progress. She may even agree to let him move ahead without everything being completely done if she could see that he was working so hard and doing well with most of it. He wasn't going to count on that though, he was planning to keep Lance focused on getting it all finished rather than having to rely on the good graces of the teacher to let him cut corners.

When they got to Maude's house, she had the table cleared off for them to work at and Ray could smell something being baked in the oven. He sorted through the papers and realized that there were fifteen units that needed to be completed. It looked like each unit had between five and seven sections. They weren't long sections, most only had ten to fifteen problems, some were even less because they were story problems. If they could complete two or three units a day, they would have the math done in about a week or just over that. He told Lance that he wanted to try for three units a day but, if it was okay with Maude, they could take a cookie and milk break along the way and then have another cookie when they completed their units for the day.

Lance agreed with that plan, and they set out working on the first unit that needed to be done.

It didn't take Ray long to realize that the goal of three units wasn't going to be at all difficult for Lance when it came to math. It was obviously his strong suit. He enjoyed the subject, and he did well with it. They stopped for a cookie and milk about halfway through the second unit and then had another when three units were completed. It was still fairly early so Ray set out a challenge. "How about we try for four unit's tomorrow? That makes it easier to divide when we're halfway done to stop for a cookie"

"Okay, that way we get math done sooner and can move to something else." Lance agreed. "I really want to make it all up so I can be with my friends."

Since they were done early, they went and sat out on the large porch where Maude had a swing and a few chairs. Ray wasn't sure that Lance would want to talk about his mom, but he was going to give it a shot. "So, your mom didn't stay at the picnic very long the other day. I was hoping to get a chance to get to know her more."

"Yeah." Lance said he hesitated and added, "It's because of the drugs."

You could have hit Ray upside the head with a frying pan, and it wouldn't have been more of a shock than Lances' confession had been. He assumed that the boy had an idea of what was going on, but he wasn't sure that he would be that open and honest about it. "Yeah, I wondered if maybe that was the problem." Ray said, he didn't want to ask questions, he wanted to leave it open ended so that Lance could volunteer whatever amount of information he was willing to share.

"She started taking stuff after we found out about my dad." Lance said softly. "I want her to get help, but I don't know if there's anything I can do."

"Well, maybe your Aunt Sally and I can help with that too." Ray offered. "I'll talk to some people that I know and see if we can figure out a way to get your mom help. But I promise you that you will always be safe. If your mom ever seems scary or sick or out of control, you come to me or your aunt and uncle, okay?"

"Okay." Lance agreed. He was quiet for a long time and that was understandable, Ray was pretty sure he had a lot on his mind after having confessed something that he had probably understood was supposed to be a secret.

After sitting for a while, Ray said, “We should probably go check on Lucky and then grab some dinner.”

“Yeah, he probably wondered where I was this afternoon.” Lance said.

“Maybe, but he’ll be happy that you come to see him now. And that will help him see that even if you can’t be with him all day, he can still count on you to make sure he gets fed. That way when school starts in the Fall, he’ll be used to you not always being there.”

“That makes sense.” Lance said. “I hope he’s my dog by then though. It would be great if I could start school telling everyone I have a dog.”

They drove to the park even though it wasn’t that far away because that would make it easier to deal with the food and the dish. When they pulled up, Lucky was over near the line of trees at the edge of the park. He didn’t stand up to come and greet them, but his tail was wagging, and he had perked up his ears. Ray filled the bowl with food and gave it to Lance. “Walk over there, slowly, see how close he lets you get before he gets anxious. Hold the bowl out in front of you so he is clear about what you’re doing. If he starts to act scared, stop, set down the bowl and step back. But go as close as he will let you without him getting spooked.”

Lance followed Ray’s instructions and was able to get close enough to stand just two feet away from the dog before he started getting antsy. He set the bowl down and took two steps back and sat down on the ground and talked softly to the dog. “It’s okay, Lucky, I’m not going to hurt you. You know me by now. Sorry I wasn’t here to hang out with you this afternoon, but I have some schoolwork I gotta catch up on. I probably won’t be here as much anymore. Once I get all this stuff done, I’m going to be going back to school. I’ll still make sure you get fed though, somehow, I’m not sure how once Ray leaves, but I’ll figure it out.” He sat and watched the dog eating and added “Maybe I can get a job mowing lawns or something but, I’ll make sure you have food. I won’t let you go hungry.”

That would be another thing that Ray would have to work out before he left town. He was pretty sure that Sally would be fine with taking in the dog if she took in Lance, but the problem would come if that plan didn’t go smoothly. He really hoped it would go well, but if Hope didn't agree to get help, his hands may be tied. He had to keep telling himself that even if she didn't agree to get help, protecting Lance was the most important thing. So far, he hadn't had any real repercussions from his mom being on drugs, he had been fortunate. His aunt and others in this small town had been looking out for him and making sure he got fed and cared for. The problem was that the longer it went on, the less likely it was that everyone could cover for her, and Lance would be the one to suffer. He hoped that no matter which way it went, the boy wouldn't end up being hateful or resentful.

They made sure Lucky got all of his food and water before they went to the diner to have a meal. When they arrived, they sat in a booth and when Sally made her way over to them, he said, "Lance knocked it out of the park today. He got three units of math done, and he's agreed to try for four tomorrow. At this rate, math will be finished in no time, and we can move on to the next subject."

"That's great news, guess that means a celebration is in order." Sally said, "Dinner and desert are on me tonight." She looked at Ray and sort of winked. "Do you need menus, or do you know what you want? Today's special is white chicken chili."

"Oh, that chili sounds great, I'll have that" Ray said somewhat excitedly.

Lance looked like he was deep in thought about what he wanted. Most likely, the chili wasn't something he had had before and wouldn't be sure if he would like it.

"Why don't you try the chili Lance, and if you don't like it, I'll buy you anything you want to replace it" Ray offered.

"Deal." Lance said. "Can I have chocolate milk?"

"Sure, what would you like to drink, Ray?"

"I'll have iced tea with lemon please." Ray said.

Sally walked away and Ray decided to ask Lance a few questions. "How well do you like your aunt and uncle. Have you spent much time with them besides here at the diner?"

“We used to, my mom and dad and I went there a lot.” Lance said somberly. “We used to have family picnics and stuff. We all used to go to the lake together.”

“I know it’s hard not having your dad, but if your mom got sick or had to go to the hospital or something like that, would you feel okay staying with them for a while?”

“Yeah, but I hope my mom doesn’t get any sicker.” he said.

“I don’t think she will, but it may be good for her to get help with the problems she has now.” Ray offered.

“You mean the drugs.” Lance said softly.

“Right. If your mom could get help with that, you’d be okay if you had to stay with them for a while?

“Um hmm.” Lance mumbled. It was obvious that he didn’t want his mom to go away, no little kid would.

“Wouldn’t it be better for her to get help now, rather than be like she is for a long time?” Ray asked.

“I know it would, but I’d really miss her.” Lance said. “I don’t think she wants to go anywhere anyway. She doesn’t like to leave the house much.”

Ray decided it was best to drop it for now. Lance wouldn’t understand just what it could mean if his mom truly got help and it would only stress him out worse if he was forced to keep talking about it.

Sally brought them their beverages and gave Ray a puzzled look, she could see that there had been a change in Lance’s demeaner, but she didn’t know what had caused it. Ray just gave a brief nod and hoped she would understand that he would talk to her more about it later. She went back to her duties since another table had just filled, but Ray was sure she would want more details later. He wasn’t going to put any plan in motion until he had talked to his friends back in LA to make sure it wouldn’t all go south on him if he did end up reporting the drug use. As much as he wanted Lance protected, he would find other ways to do it if the system was going to let them down. If nothing else, he would see if he could get Lance’s mom to sign some sort of papers giving Sally and Steve the rights to take Lance for medical treatment and other things as needed so that even if she wouldn't go to rehab at least his relatives could step in and make sure the boy was cared for.

When Sally brought the chili, she also had a large bowl of tortilla chips, Lance looked at both rather puzzled. Ray picked up a tortilla chip and dipped it into the chili, scooping out a good sized bite, blew on it and then put it in his mouth. "Mmmm, this is good." Ray said. "You should try it, it's best with the chips, almost like a dip."

Lance tentatively picked up a chip and dipped it into the bowl. He blew on it just as Ray had and then took a small bite. He looked very pensive as he chewed, almost as if he was sure at some point he would realize that he didn't like it, but he continued to chew and eventually swallow.

"Well, what do you think?" Ray asked.

"It's good, it looks weird, but it tastes pretty good." Lance said, scooping more with the rest of his chip.

"See, that's the thing in life, Lance, sometimes things don't look or sound good to us, but we should still give it a try. We may like it a lot more than we think we will." Ray said.

They both finished their dinner and Lance decided that he wanted to go back and spend some more time with Lucky. "Don't stay out too late thought, we have lots of work to do tomorrow." Ray cautioned. "Head home before it gets dark."

"Okay." Lance said and then raced out of the restaurant in the direction of the park.

Sally came over to clear the table and Ray said "Lance told me today that his mom misses out on a lot of things because of the drugs. I guess it kind of took me by surprise that he knew about it or more so that he was so open and honest about it all. I would have thought a kid like that wouldn't understand or at least wouldn't feel comfortable talking about it all. But that's not the case. That worries me because if it becomes something that he just sees as part of life, I'm afraid that makes it easier to go down that path himself."

"Yeah, I get what you mean, but we have to be careful, he can't lose any more people and I know you don't plan to stay around forever." Sally said.

"Well, I don't plan to leave until something is settled for Lance and I have some other things I'm working on too, including the tablet for Maude. That should be getting here any day now and I have to get the software and stuff set up and connect her to her family." Ray said. "I'll be here for a while yet."

"I just hope it will be okay for Lance if you leave."

"I'll make sure he's on solid ground before I go." Ray promised. Sally walked away, so Ray stepped outside and went to his SUV. This was a conversation he didn't need anyone in this small town hearing until the details were worked out for the best possible solution.

When the man picked up on the other end, Ray said "Hey Mike. This is Ray. I have a couple of questions for you. Well, technically they're for your wife, but I had your number, so I was hoping you could pass things along."

"Sure, what's up?" Mike asked.

"I'm in a small town a few hundred miles outside of LA, so it's not in the county, it is in the state though, so I figured the same laws would apply." Ray explained. "Hypothetically, if there was a young mom that is having problems with substance abuse, and she has a kid that's around eleven, what are the options for the kid being able to be placed with a family member if the mom gets help."

"Well, part of your situation I can answer. The courts always prefer a placement with a family member if one is available." Mike said. "I can't say much about the situation with the mom though. If there's a drug connection, law enforcement may get involved and it won't be pretty."

"That's what I'm hoping to avoid, if possible." Ray said. "If we can get the mom to go to rehab willingly, I'm hoping we can put a temporary guardianship or foster care or something with an aunt and uncle that live in the same town. It's a small town, everyone knows everyone type of thing. I'd like to keep it as simple as possible and not involve law enforcement. But the kid is the main concern. I want him covered even if crap does go downhill for his mom. The aunt and uncle are willing to take him in for however long they need to, but a stint in rehab for ninety days would be far better than however many years she might get for possession. And that's if it's just possession. I don't know her much, she stays out of public for the most part, but I can't guarantee that she's not selling or distributing for someone who is selling."

"Well, Becca's not home yet, but I'll tell her you called. And by the way, she isn't in the same position, she got promoted so she might actually be more help. She covers most of the state now, so not being in the county may not be an issue." Mike said.

"That's great, feel free to call me or have her call me anytime." Ray said. He disconnected the call and headed to Maude's for his nightly ritual of game shows and chamomile tea. He was kind of starting to like the simple life of this small town. He still had the desire to see more of the country, but he wasn't in any hurry.

He settled into the big chair next to Maude's and watched one game show before his phone rang. It was a number he didn't recognize, but it definitely had the LA prefix, so he excused himself to take the call out on the porch. "Hello."

"Hello, Ray, it's Becca." the woman said. "Mike told me you needed me to call. He gave me a little bit of the background, but why don't you fill me in."

"First, I don't want to mess you up in a professional capacity, but can this be off the record?" Ray asked. "At least for now?"

"I'm pretty sure it can be, unless you tell me a child is being abused, I am not required to say anything and if you can personally assure me that there are people that would step in if anything got worse, I'll keep it between you and I for now." Becca assured. "Besides, I don't know exactly where you are so I can't really track you down."

"Okay, so I met this kid here and I don't know there was just something about him that intrigued me. He seemed like a loner; except he's trying to befriend this stray dog that hangs around. The more time I spent with him, the more I liked him." Ray began. "He's like the only kid in this town that didn't get to go to summer camp this year. All his friends got to go. He's going to be held back in school unless he can make up a bunch of work, which I'm helping him do. He wants to pass so badly because all of his friends are going up a grade."

"I get that you want to help a kid, but if he's not doing his schoolwork, you helping him may only push the problem back a year." Becca said.

"No, see the thing is, a few months ago, his dad got killed in action. I don't know all the details of that, but that's when his schoolwork and school attendance started to suffer." Ray explained.

"Oh, yeah, that is different then." Becca agreed.

"Here's where my concern comes in and would like your input." he began. "About that same time, I'm pretty sure his mom starting using drugs. Heck, I don't know, she may have used them before to some degree, but I think that's what pushed her over the edge to either start or to increase her usage."

"What kind of drugs are we talking?" Becca asked.

"I don't know for sure; my guess would be heroine or it could be meth I suppose. The one time I met her, she looked like her clothes were too big like maybe she lost weight and she was wearing a long sleeved shirt to a town picnic on a hot summer day in Southern California, so I'm thinking she may have track marks and is trying to hide them. I'm not positive what her drug of choice is though, but I do know there's some type of drug involved."

"Does she neglect the kid." the woman asked.

"I think she just pretty much lets him do what he wants. Fortunately, his aunt and uncle own the only diner in town, and they make sure he gets fed. Well, now that I'm here, I'm helping with that some too, but they've been doing it for a while." Ray said.

"So, what is your hope for the situation?"

"Well, the aunt and uncle are willing to become temporary guardians or foster parents or whatever. My preference would be that we get the mom to voluntarily go into rehab and sign some documents saying that the aunt and uncle can take care of him until a time when she is better." Ray took a deep breath and then continued, "If she won't go voluntarily, I'm hoping that we can make sure the child is protected in the event that she does get arrested or have other complications that would make her unable to care for the child." He realized he hadn't told her Lance's name, there was just something about this whole thing that made him want to protect that information as long as he possibly could.

"Well, fortunately, the system still prefers blood over stranger. If there is a relative that lives in the same school district it's pretty easy, some times the courts don't want to switch schools if it can be helped, but this situation sounds ideal." Becca said. "I assume the aunt and uncle are of an age where a judge wouldn't question that placement if it had to go through the courts?"

"Yeah, they're probably in their 30's and they own the diner, so they have at least a decent income." Ray said.

"You'd be surprised how little judges worry about income, I mean they can't be homeless or something, but the court can help with finances. They are less likely to do a placement if the aunt and uncle are very young or very old. Thirties is basically perfect though. Do they have other kids?"

"No, is that going to be a problem?" Ray asked.

"Actually, it goes in their favor. If they already had several it's more of an issue." Becca explained.

"So, what's our first step?" Ray asked.

"Well, ideally, if you can convince the mom to go into rehab the paperwork to set up the temporary guardianship is pretty easy. If she doesn't just volunteer to go, it can still be easy to set up the guardianship, but I may have to give you a little muscle to go with it." Becca said.

"In what way?" Ray asked.

"Well, you'd be amazed at what happens when CPS or something similar gets invited to the intervention." Becca said. "People seem more likely to agree to things if they think the courts are going to take away their rights to make a choice."

"But I really don't want that to happen." Ray stated. "I don't want the courts involved if I can help it."

"Well, you try to get her to go voluntarily, and if that goes well, then you're all set." Becca said. "If not, Mike and I would love to see you again. Maybe you can take us to this diner you talk about and introduce us to this child and the mother. If you just happen to mention who I work for, she may change her mind. It might be dirty pool as they say because I won't be there in an official capacity, but she doesn't need to know that. And like I said, as long as I don't see evidence of the drugs actually in her possession, or evidence of the child being abused, I don't have to treat it as an official visit."

"So, what do we need to do?" Ray asked, "As far as paperwork and all that, if she agrees."

"I'll send you a document that you can print and fill out and then send it to me, I'll make sure it gets filed in the proper places and within a few days of that, it will be official that the child's aunt and uncle are his legal guardians for the time being."

"Thanks, Becca, I appreciate it." Ray said, "Thanks for taking the time to call me back."

"It's no problem, Ray. Let me know if you need any other information." Becca said. "Take care and I'll talk to you soon."

"You take care too, bye Becca." Ray hung up his phone. He had a lot of thinking to do. He wanted Hope to get help, but he didn't want Lance to resent him in the process.

# Chapter 7

The following morning, Maude could tell that something was still bugging Ray. She figured it was the phone call he had taken last night because he had been pretty quiet when they shared their tea, but this morning he still seemed to have a lot on his mind, or a heavy heart about something. At first, she wasn't going to meddle, but she realized that he was doing a lot of meddling into her business, oh, she was glad that he was, but still, maybe it gave her just a little bit of a right to put her nose in his business too. "You've seemed a thousand miles away since that phone call last night, I hope it wasn't bad news." she said while pouring coffee into each of their cups.

"No, I'm just considering doing something that might not make some people very happy with me." Ray stated.

"Is it something that's for their own good, even if they don't see it that way?" Maude asked.

"It is." Ray said succinctly.

"Oh, Ray." she began. "I've been the villain more times than I can count because I've made those same choices. As a momma, there were hundreds, maybe even thousands of times that my children were absolutely sure I was out to ruin their lives. Every time I made them be home for a curfew or told them they couldn't go to one place or another or that they couldn't hang out with certain people, they hated me for it. But in the end, they've grown up and they've realized that I wasn't a tyrant, I was just protecting them from dangers they didn't even know were out there."

"Does it always take that long?" Ray asked.

“No, not always.” Maude replied. “There were many things that they understood a lot quicker, but as a parent, it’s an ongoing thing. Their daddy and I had to tell them no many times. Some of them they came around on a lot sooner than others, but eventually, they always see that it was done in their best interest. Now that they have children of their own, every single one of them has come back to me and told me that they appreciated those things even though they didn’t think they would at the time.”

Ray continued to eat mostly in silence other than responding when Maude asked if he wanted more of something. His brain was just too consumed with the possibilities. Would Lance hate him? Would Hope take the easier route, or was it going to have to get messy before she would get help? And if they did have to get CPS or law enforcement involved, would that make everyone in town think he was sticking his nose where it didn’t belong? He almost didn’t notice when his phone rang, he probably would have missed it altogether if Maude hadn’t said something. He looked at the caller ID and was surprised to see that it was Becca again. “Hello.” he said, standing to go to the other room, he wasn’t sure he was ready for Maude to hear his phone conversation since it was going to be a touchy subject.

“Hey, Ray.” Becca said. “You said you’re still in Cali, right?”

“Yeah.”

“I made an appointment for you for tomorrow at a place just north of San Bernadino. It’s the best rehab facility I know. They may be able to offer you some insight as to how to approach your friend and they would know far more than I do about cost and insurance. Her husband’s VA stuff may come in to play, or not, I don’t know. But they have the best success rate in the area. I figured it can’t hurt to at least sit down and talk with them and get some ideas on how to proceed.” She paused and then said, “They have your name, so if tomorrow doesn’t work, just give them a call and reschedule. I’ll text you the number and address.”

“That would be great, thanks.” Ray said. A few moments after he hung up the call, the text came through. It wouldn’t hurt to at least go and talk to the person at the rehab place, maybe they could even offer him other options.

When he went to the park after finishing his breakfast, Lance and Lucky were there waiting for him as usual. Ray decided not to say anything about his trip tomorrow until they were studying later. They fed Lucky and then he asked Lance if he wanted to go play basketball or maybe try some baseball.

"We can't really play baseball with just the two of us." Lance said.

"Sure, we can." Ray said. "We can play catch, or we can work on batting practice. We can't play a full game with running bases and all that, but we can work to improve our skills. It's like your schoolwork, you won't ever get better if you don't keep working on it. Sports are the same way, the more you practice the better you get. Anyone can run bases but batting and pitching and catching are things you can work to get better at."

"Yeah, that's true." Lance agreed. "Do you think we should go to the school to play catch? I don't want to scare Lucky."

"Let's see how it goes here, if he seems to get scared by it, we'll move." Ray had a theory, but he wasn't going to tell Lance what it was until he had something to go on. He went and got the baseball equipment he had bought out of his SUV. He handed Lance the youth sized baseball mitt and put his own glove on his left hand. They moved over to an open area in the park and started throwing the ball back and forth. Both Ray and Lance kept glancing at Lucky to gage his reaction. He didn't seem scared, in fact, he seemed intrigued.

The next time Ray caught the ball, he paused for a minute and said to Lance, "The next time you get the ball, don't throw it towards me, throw it towards Lucky. Not close enough he might be afraid it's going to hit him, but close enough that he knows it's his turn to get the ball. We'll see what he does."

When Lance had the ball, he gave it a toss in Lucky's direction. The dog paused for a minute as if he were unsure of what to do, but he eventually took the steps needed to pick up the ball. He brought it towards Lance and dropped it on the ground about two feet away from the boy. He then sat and looked at his friend expectantly. Lance looked at Ray with total excitement in his eyes.

"Toss it a little way away, but make sure he can watch where it goes. Don't throw it hard or fast." Ray said. Lance followed his instruction and that was when Ray realized that the dog had definitely had a kind and loving owner in his past somewhere. But like happens to so many animals and even to some people, someone failed him along the way, and he became guarded and afraid to trust. They had no way of ever knowing what that tragedy had been, but they could help him learn to love and trust again.

Ray took off his glove and went to sit on one of the picnic tables, he didn't want to interfere with the two while they bonded over a game of fetch. It seemed like he had accomplished one of his goals for the people in this town. Oh, he knew it would most likely still take time before Lucky was fully ready to go home with Lance or be ready for a collar or any sign of ownership, but if he was playing fetch, it was definitely a step in the right direction.

They played for several more rounds and each time, Lucky brought the ball close, but not close enough that Lance could have reached out to grab him. Finally, both dog and boy seemed to be wearing out. Ray went over and turned on the water faucet and after rinsing the bowl, he sat it down to let it fill up. Once he had stepped back away, the dog trotted over happily lapping up the cool refreshment.

"You ready to go grab some lunch and then get started on your homework?" Ray asked.

Lance took one last look towards Lucky and then said "Sure."

When they got to Sally's, Lance was excited to tell his aunt, "Aunt Sally, my dog and I played fetch today and he's really good at it."

Sally gave Ray a quizzical look over the top of Lance's head. So Ray explained, "Yep, they played a good game of fetch. The dog's still a little timid, he doesn't often get too close, but fetch seemed to be something he's familiar with." He gave a small shrug, he didn't fully know what Sally's thoughts were going to be about the dog and he didn't want to make it seem certain that Lance was bringing a dog with him when he came to stay with her, if he came to stay with her.

They finished their lunch and made their way back to Maude's house to start working on Lance's math units. When they got two done, Ray said "Why don't we take our cookies and milk out on the front porch."

"Okay" Lance grabbed his two cookies and the milk that Maude had poured for him.

"Tomorrow, I have to go and take care of some business, so I won't be around much of the day." Ray began. "I'll make sure we get Lucky's food in the morning, and I'll be back before late, but I won't be around to help you with your schoolwork. Right now, you have six units left after today that should be down to four. If you can work on them tomorrow, it would be good. Even if you don't get four done, it would make us that much closer."

"Yeah." Lance said with no enthusiasm.

"The thing is Lance; math is obviously something you're very good at. I hardly have to help you at all with math." Ray began. "Mostly it's just staying focused, which I know can be hard to do. Do you think you would have an easier time focusing here or at the diner? I'm sure your Aunt Sally wouldn't mind you sitting in a booth and working, but I don't know if that would be distracting. I could see if Maude is okay with you coming here to work as long as you promise to not take advantage of the fact that she makes really good cookies."

"I think the diner gets noisy sometimes, and here is quiet." Lance said. "But Maude isn't my aunt or grandma or anything, so I don't know if she'll want to let me come over if you're not here."

"Well, we can ask her when we go back inside." Ray said. "You might be surprised. Maude's family all lives far away, and she might like having company sometimes."

When they finished their snack and walked back to the table, Lance sat down and got back to work quietly. Ray put their glasses in the sink after rinsing them out and then he turned to Maude. "I have to go out of town on business for a few hours tomorrow. Lance and I were wondering if maybe it would be okay for him to come here and work on his homework for a while. He could go to his aunt's diner, but you know it can get noisy at a place like that at times. Would you mind if he worked on things at your table? He generally doesn't need a lot of help with math, but from what I've seen you're pretty good at most subjects. At least if your game show watching is any indication."

"Oh, I'd love to have him come by." Maude said. She turned to Lance and added, "Lance you're welcome here in my home anytime. If you ever need a friend or a place to be, you come and knock on my door. I'd love to have the company. My grandchildren live far away. It would be nice to have you stop by and I promise if you come by, I'll always have cookies or something we can have for a treat. They may not always be homemade if I don't know you're coming, but I'll keep things on hand just for us."

"That would be great." Lance said. "I don't really have any grandmas either."

"Well, people don't have to be related by blood to treat each other like family." Maude stated. She gave him a wink and then said, "You get back to your work now, so you have some time to go play after your units are done."

At the end of the day, Lance had four units of math left. Ray told him to try to get them done, but if he couldn't it was okay. There was no pressure, they had time. Ray wasn't sure if things would go well with the change or not and he didn't want Lance to beat himself up if he just couldn't work as well.

# Chapter 8

The following morning, Ray didn't eat much of his breakfast, there were just too many things on his mind. "You feeling alright this morning, Ray?" Maude asked.

"Yeah, just this business trip I have to make, I've got a lot on my mind I guess." he replied.

"I hope it's not anything bad." she stated.

Ray got the feeling that she was trying to pry without seeming like she was prying. Which was okay, he understood her position. It was a small town, he was living in her home, they had become friends of sorts over the time he had been staying here. He just wasn't sure how anyone would feel about what he was planning to do with his day. He knew that Maude could be the biggest gossip in town, but he also knew she was trustworthy. He decided to take a chance and get someone else's opinion of what he was about to do. "I don't know if it's going to be bad or not, Maude. I hope it's going to turn out good, but I may not make some people very happy with me in the process."

"Oh?" that was all Maude said, but the one word spoke volumes about her curiosity.

"I'm going to a rehab facility near San Bernadino to get some advice on how to try to get help for Lance's mom." He didn't say anymore, and that statement hung in the air for a long while.

"I hope you get the answers you need, Ray." she began. "I do know that someone needs to do something. I'm not sure that she will be willing to get help, but someone has to try. I've seen her go from a vibrant young mother to a recluse in less than a year. I don't know for sure that she uses drugs, I can't personally speak to things I haven't seen with my own eyes. But the things I do see and hear make me think that it is likely that she does."

"That's how I feel too, although Lance did say something about his mom being the way she is because of the drugs." Ray said. "I think that's my biggest motivation in all of this, if Lance knows she's doing drugs, how long before it goes further, will he want to experiment with them, will she get even deeper and possibly even overdose. Those are things I have to try to stop if I can."

"You're a good soul Ray." Maude said.

"Thank you." Ray replied. "My biggest fear is what to do if she says no to getting help. I still want to protect Lance, but that route could get ugly and if it does, will Lance hate me for it?"

"Oh, that's one of those things that parents learn quick." Maude said. "Like I told you before, my kids hated me for sure many times over. Lance may think he hates you if his mom goes away, but if she comes back and can be in his life again, he won't hold any hard feelings. Sometimes being the parent or in this case, the responsible adult is hard, but if the end justifies the means, it's worth it."

"I hope so" Ray said. "I really hope she agrees to go willingly. If she doesn't, I don't know that it would be effective anyway."

Ray finished his coffee and then went to the park to make sure Lance had the dish and food for Lucky. When he saw the boy he asked, "Lance, we've become pretty good friends, right?"

"Yeah." Lance said confused.

"If I were to do something you didn't like, do you think you would be able to forgive me?"

Lance seemed to think about that for a long time before saying "I guess it kind of depends on what it was that you did. I mean if you accidently hit me or something, I'd forgive you right away because it was an accident. But if you tried to hurt me to be mean, then that's different."

Ray wasn't sure how to explain himself, but he wanted to try. "Okay, let's say I did do it on purpose, but for a good reason. Like if I found out that Lucky was sick, and I told you that you couldn't hang out with him until we could get him better. Would you hate me for that?"

"Do you think Lucky is sick?" Lance asked.

"No, I'm just trying to think of an example." Ray promised.

"Well, I guess I'd have to say it depends." Lance said. "Like if he's sick but maybe I could help him, then I'd be mad that you wouldn't let me help him. But if he's sick and needs to go to a doctor then I wouldn't be mad that you wouldn't let me try to take care of him. Would you help me take him to the doctor though?"

"Oh, Lance," Ray said getting a little choked up. "I'd do anything in my power to get him better if he'd let me. If he wouldn't come to me, I might have to try to figure out a way to trap him, and that would maybe make him more scared for a while, but it would be for his best interest if he got better, right?"

"Yeah, I would want him to get better because I want him to be my dog." Lance agreed.

"Great, that's just great." Ray stated. At least he hoped that Lance would feel the same way about his mom getting help.

They hung out long enough for Lucky to get his food and water, but then Ray needed to go. "I need to get headed to my meeting. Don't stay out here so long that you forget your lunch or your schoolwork. I'll be back in time for dinner and feeding Lucky again. Okay?"

"Okay." Lance didn't seem overly excited about it, but he was resolved to the fact that Ray would be back, and he needed to make the most of his day.

When Ray arrived at the rehab facility, he was impressed, it didn't look like some clinical hospital that was drab and dreary. It looked more like a huge home. He walked into the large foyer and was greeted by a young woman behind a desk. "Hello, may I help you?"

"I have an appointment with Kelly, I believe. I'm Ray Hawthorne."

"Of course, if you'll have a seat, I'll let her know you're here."

Ray sat on one of the large comfortable chairs and looked around. The place seemed to have maybe been a home at one point in time, although if it had, it had belonged to someone very wealthy because it was huge from what he could see. It had only been a couple of minutes when a woman who was probably in her early forties came through the archway that led to the rest of the building. She approached Ray and held out her hand "Hello, Ray, I'm Kelly."

Ray had stood when he saw the woman approaching and shook her hand "I appreciate you taking the time to meet with me and answer my questions."

She guided him down a short hallway to an office. "Please, have a seat." she said as she closed the door. "So, Becca told me a little bit about why you wanted to meet with me, but why don't you fill me in on the details."

"Well, I've recently started traveling around mostly to take photos for a few travel magazines, and I stopped in a small town over near Joshua Tree. Anyway, I kept seeing this kid hanging around town, but other than this stray dog he's trying to win over, I never really saw him with anyone, so I was curious."

She nodded so he continued, "Anyway, I found out that all the other kids his age are off to camp, and he used to go, but not this year, so I asked him why. He told me his dad died in the military a few months ago so his mom didn't get it set up for him to go to camp this year. There's a lot more to all of it, but over the course of time, I've pieced together the fact that the mom has been using drugs to try to help with her grief."

"Do you know what drugs?" Kelly asked.

"No, my guess would be heroine or meth, at least something that she injects. I've only met her once at a town picnic and she was wearing long sleeves. It had to have been in the nineties that day. Her clothes don't fit her right, like maybe she's lost weight. Her hair is, I don't know, it looked clean, but not healthy if that makes sense. And she didn't stay long at all, mostly just came so she could meet me because I think her son was begging her too, but she left right after. And, the other day, Lance made a comment about his mom not really being fully available because of the drugs. So, he at least knows she's doing them, how much of it all he sees, I don't know. He's a pretty smart kid although he's not going to go onto the next grade unless he can get a lot of schoolwork caught up. I think after his dad died, his mom didn't really put a lot of emphasis on going to school and keeping up with homework and the kid probably didn't really feel like doing it either. We've got a few people in town that are trying to help him get caught up on the missed assignments though."

"Sounds like there's a great support system in place, does she have any family?" Kelly asked.

"Lance has an aunt and an uncle, but they are from his father's side, and they are more than willing to take care of him if she does decide to go into rehab. No one seems to know much else about her family other than the fact that Lance did say he doesn't really have any grandmas."

"Do you think she would go into rehab willingly?" she asked.

"I really don't know." Ray began, "like I said, I haven't really talked to her at all. I don't think anyone has known how to confront her or whatever, but I think we've all realized something needs to be done. I guess I was hoping that you could give me some pointers on what and how to ask. What the program is like when she can start if she's willing. How long does she have to be here? Things like that, I am hoping that I can go and talk to her and tell her what's available and she jumps at the opportunity to get better. Although I know that's probably not very likely. Becca did say that if needed she could make some unofficial visits or whatever to push Hope towards getting help. I'd rather not scare the woman into thinking that she could lose her son if I can help it, but the truth of the matter is, she very well may lose him if she keeps going down this road."

"Well, it's admirable that you want to help them, and you are right, if she doesn't go into rehab, whether it be here or somewhere else, she may very well lose her child and potentially everything else. Does she own a home?"

"I don't know if she owns or rents, she has a small house." Ray replied.

"Well, either way, generally if addicts don't get help, they tend to lose their living space and everything else." Kelly stated. "So, here's what we offer. Our program is ninety days from start to finish. That's not to say that everyone is out the door on day ninety-one and that's also not to say that everyone is here for the full ninety. If people don't want to be here, we won't make them. Even if its court ordered, we aren't the ones that enforce that. If someone wants to walk, they walk. On the other end, if there's someone who's had a few setbacks but is honestly trying, we aren't going to say 'your program is up time to leave'".

"That's good to know." Ray said.

"While here, there are lots of classes and groups and support." Kelly said. "Some insurances pay for it, some don't. That's something that is a concern for some. If it's court ordered, then the client only pays whatever the court deems appropriate."

"I would really rather keep the courts out of it if possible. I'd much rather she agrees to let her in-laws become temporary guardians and she come here willingly." Ray said. "If her insurance doesn't cover it, we'll work on that some other way."

"Okay, well, why don't I show you around a little and explain what happens here and answer any questions that may come up along the way." Kelly said standing up from her chair. Ray followed her through the large building as she pointed out the sleeping quarters, the counseling offices, the group therapy rooms, and the kitchen and dining room.

"Do you have staff that cooks, or do the residents have to do that?" Ray asked.

"We have a head cook, but the residents rotate jobs. The first week or two is really all about getting them clean and giving them a new focus, but once the drugs are out of their system, they get assigned things like cooking, dishes, cleaning, laundry. Each person washes their own clothing, again, after that initial period, so laundry duty would consist more of the dishtowels, and towels and bedding of staff who live on site."

"So, there's always staff present?" Ray asked.

"There are. This is an all woman's facility, so live in staff are all female. We do have a few male counselors that come in because some people do better talking to one gender or the other, but no males are here after regular hours. It just keeps everything above board so to speak."

"I'm sure that's a good policy to have."

"Well, withdraw is different for everyone and while we try not to put hands on anyone, that's not always avoidable, and that way we don't have to worry about anyone saying a man did something inappropriate while trying to take them down from a violent episode."

"Do those happen a lot?"

"It really varies. What drug the person is taking, how much they've been taking, how much is still in their system. We do have medications available that often help with the symptoms, but we don't force anyone to take them." Kelly stated. "We will only administer it if the person agrees to it. The last thing we want to do is force someone who is trying to come off of drug addiction to take something into their body that they aren't okay with. Even if it is a substance that would likely help alleviate their symptoms."

After the tour, Ray asked if there was any literature he could take to read and to offer to Hope or her family if they wanted to know more. Just before he left, he checked his phone and found the document from Becca was in his email. He asked Kelly if he could print it there and when he left, he was fully armed to confront Hope. He hoped she would see the value in getting help and having her son safe with family, but if not, he was willing to reevaluate and try for an intervention. Nothing was more important than getting help for Hope and thereby keeping Lance safe.

# Chapter 9

When Ray got back to his SUV, he tucked the paperwork from the facility along with the documents from Becca into a briefcase in the back seat. He headed back to the small town to find Lance. He wasn't going to try to talk to Hope until he had a plan in place for where Lance was going to be at the time. The last thing Ray wanted was to have the boy walk in on them when they were talking about his mom giving temporary custody to his aunt and uncle and then going away for three months. If she agreed, they would all have to sit down and talk out the logistics and reassure Lance that nothing bad was going to happen and that this really was a good thing. Ray wasn't sure what that would mean for him if she did say yes. Obviously, he hoped she agreed willingly, but even if she didn't and they had to go the more difficult route, Lance was going to have a difficult time for ninety days or more. Ray knew that he would stay until Lance was okay with him leaving or until Hope was back home, he wasn't going to let him leaving be another thing that hurt Lance.

He drove by the park expecting to see Lance there, but he wasn't. Lucky was hanging out back by the line of trees at the far edge of the park. He perked up when he saw Ray's SUV but didn't move since no one stopped and no one got out. Ray drove on to Maude's house and found the boy and the older woman sitting on the front porch munching on cookies and drinking milk.

Ray parked and got out "Taking a study break?" he asked.

"Oh, no, we're all done, have been for a while." Maude replied.

"That's great, so all the math is done?" Ray queried.

"Sure is." Lance said excitedly. "Maybe we can take it to Mrs. Cooper and see what I have to work on next."

"Sounds like a plan." Ray said. "Finish your snack, I'll call to see if she's home."

When Lance had finished his milk, he and Ray walked over to the teacher's house to turn in the math assignments and pick up the things for whatever subject was next. She suggested they take Social Studies next, there were eight units to be completed. They dropped them off at Maude's house, so they were ready for the next day and then, the rest of the day went like any other, dinner at Sally's and then time at the park with Lucky.

The following morning over breakfast Maude said, "I looked over the work that Lance needs to do for his social studies. It's pretty straightforward and I'm sure I could help him if you ever need to go take pictures or whatever. I know he likes to study with you, but I'd be glad to help if you ever need some time. I don't know what all the details of this plan you've got going on, but I know when something's brewing and I just wanted to offer if you need me, I'm here. I think Lance and I get on okay."

"Thanks, Maude." Ray said. "I appreciate that. I'll see how Lance feels about it."

He met Lance at the park and found the boy sitting with the dog not three feet away, waiting for his breakfast. He grabbed the food and the bowl and headed over to them. He sat on the other side of Lance and passed him the filled bowl so he could put it by Lucky.

After several minutes, he asked, "So, how was it studying with Maude yesterday?"

"It was good, she's really smart." Lance said. "She's kind of like a grandma, you know?"

"Yeah, well, Maude is a grandma, not your grandma of course, but she does have grandkids, so she probably likes having you come over" Ray said.

"Yeah, I think maybe she's lonely." Lance said. "I mean not right now, because you live there, and I come over to do school work, but maybe when you have to go to your next place, maybe I'll go see her sometimes."

“Maybe when school starts, she can help you with homework if you need it.” Ray offered.

“Yeah, that would be good.” Lance agreed. “My mom usually doesn’t feel like helping me, that’s why I got behind last year. I could have done better though, I don’t usually need someone to help me much, but I think with my dad and all that, I didn’t feel like doing my work.”

“That’s totally understandable, Lance.” Ray said. “That’s why your teacher is giving you the chance to make things up. She knows you didn’t just stop working because you wanted to be a bad kid. She knows that something bad made you just not feel like working for a while. But now you’re getting back on track and stepping up and taking responsibility for what needs to be done. People notice things like that in life, Lance. They know when you’re really making an effort to make things better.”

“Yeah.” was all Lance said.

Ray looked over and realized that the dog dish was empty, and Lucky had picked it up and walked it closer to Lance and set it down. “Just like Lucky there, he knows you’ll take care of him, see he brought you the dish so you can get him some water.”

Lance looked up and saw the dish next to him. He picked it up and said “Good boy Lucky. Are you thirsty, do you want water?” He stood up slowly and picked up the dish. He walked over to the water faucet and the dog followed a few paces behind. He rinsed out the dish and then filled it with the cool water. He sat it down a foot away from him and said, “Go ahead boy, you know I won’t hurt you. Go ahead and take a drink.”

The dog had his head lowered, but kept his eyes firmly on Lance, just in case, but he slowly eased towards the cold liquid and started lapping it up, slowly at first, but his speed increased the more sure he became that Lance wasn’t going to move any closer to him. When he had his fill, he walked back over towards the woods so he could lay in the shade. Lance made his way back over to Ray.

“I think Lucky is getting less scared of me.” he said.

“I do too.” Ray agreed. “It’s hard to figure out what’s going on in his head. He played fetch with you and that tells me he had a person that he’s done that with before. Someone he trusted. But then something made him not sure that all humans were okay. I'm not sure of the reason for it, but he is learning that you won't hurt him and that's a good thing."

They sat for a while longer just talking about some of Lance's friends who were away at camp and when they would be home. He talked about what teachers he hoped to get next year if he finished his work so that he could move forward. He didn't really ever talk much about his mom or his dad, it was probably something that was hard for him to discuss.

When they got hungry, they went to grab lunch and then went to Maude's to get started on the social studies units. These units were more complex, they required reading a section and then answering several questions about the things that had been read, so they set a goal of two a day with a snack break after one. Although Ray was there and pitched in, it was obvious that this was a topic that Maude loved. She often chimed in and eventually, she was sitting with them and helping find the answers needed.

That gave Ray an idea. When they were done for the day and the three of them were sitting on the porch enjoying their cookie and milk, Ray decided to toss his thoughts out there. "So, Lance, I have a few things I'd like to do tomorrow afternoon, and I was wondering how you would feel about working with Maude for a day. Actually, I think she knows way more about social studies than I do and is probably a better helper anyway."

"Sure." Lance agreed happily. "I like studying with her. Will you be gone all day though?"

"No, we'll have lunch and then you can head here, and I'll go take care of my stuff and we'll meet after, okay?"

"Okay."

They went to the school to play a little basketball since it wasn't time for dinner yet. Ray was working on helping Lance get better at any sports. It would be something a dad would do if he were still here, but in his absence, Ray wanted the boy to feel comfortable when his friends asked him to play a game of ball.

They ended their day in the same manner as all others, having their meal and then making sure Lucky got his. It wasn't late, so Lance asked if he could play some fetch with Lucky with Ray's baseball. Ray agreed and the game lasted until dusk. Ray promised to meet Lance in the park the following day.

The day started off like every other. But when Lance sat down at the table to work with Maude, Ray excused himself. He was going to go and see if he could find Hope at home.

He knocked on the door of the house. It wasn't large, but it looked like a decent size for a small family. He knocked a second time when he thought he heard movement inside. Eventually, Hope opened the door. She was obviously surprised to see him. "Uh, Lance isn't here."

"I know, I left him with Maude working on some of his make-up work for school." Ray said. "Can I come in? I have something I'd like to talk to you about." He had the file folder in his hand. He hoped he could get her to see the benefit of doing this the voluntary way, but if he couldn't, he would go the forceful route if he had to.

"Um, sure." Hope said.

Ray looked around and it somewhat surprised him that the house was clean. Not immaculate, but with a boy Lance's age, he didn't expect it to be. He had been afraid that with her addiction Hope may not have been taking care of the house, she definitely wasn't taking responsibility for feeding her child. On the other hand, Ray realized that it was very possible that Lance was doing most of or all of the cleaning and chores around the house because he realized that his mom needed help.

Hope seemed very nervous when she invited him to sit down. He chose a seat on the couch that had a small coffee table in front of it. He could lay out the brochure and other paperwork there for her to see. She sat at the other end of the couch. She was stiff as a board as she sat. She was very like anticipating an attack or accusations and while he was going to be honest about what he knew, he was hoping he could do it with kindness.

"Hope." Ray began. He hesitated until she looked at him and then he continued, "I think you may have a problem, and I'd like to help you with that. I'd like to help you get better so that you can be a better mom for Lance."

"I'm trying to be a good mom." she said, she sounded a little choked up or unsure of her words.

"I know, you're trying. But I think that your grief and the loss of your husband made you go down a path you wouldn't have gone down otherwise and it's affecting a lot of things in your life." He paused to see if she had any reaction. She did, she pulled her sleeves further down her arm. She had understood exactly what he was referring to. "Hope, I don't want to be harsh about this. I want to get you help. Or more accurately, I want to help you get help for yourself and for Lance."

"I need to be here, so Lance has a home." Hope argued.

"Hope, again, I'm not trying to be mean here, but he has a place to sleep and not much else from you right now." Ray stated. "He eats at Sally's; Maude and I have been helping him catch up on the schoolwork he missed from last year so that he can move forward with his friends. Look, even Lance has told me that you are the way you are because of the drugs. He's a kid, Hope, and even he sees that you have a problem."

"But if I went away, what would happen to him?"

"Well, Sally and Steve have agreed to take him for however long you need to be gone. This paper would give them temporary guardianship. It would make it so that they can seek medical care if he needs it, they could sign papers and things for the school, and he could stay with them until you get better and get back home." He handed her the three page document and she began reading it.

It took her close to an hour to go through the paperwork, she went back through a few times to be sure exactly what she was reading. "And if I agree to let them keep him, what happens to me?"

"Well, I'm hoping that you will consider going to a rehabilitation facility near San Bernadino. I visited there the other day at the recommendation of a friend and it's a great place with a very high success rate. I have their brochures here and can answer any questions or if I can't, I will contact someone who can." He pushed the information towards her on the table. She picked it up and started scanning through it.

"It's in a big house, rather than some medical type of facility. It's really a nice place." Ray said. "It's all women at this facility other than some male counselors that come in for appointments or groups. But no men live there." He was trying to think of anything that might be a selling point to her.

She continued to go through the pamphlet and brochures. At least she hadn't thrown them at him and told him to get out. That was a plus for sure. He didn't want to pressure her, but he had been here almost two hours already with the time it was taking her to read through everything and he was sure she was doing a lot of thinking as she read too.

When it seemed like maybe she was through the stack of information, Ray decided to try one more time. "They said some insurance covers it, some doesn't, but if yours doesn't, we can work out a way to pay for the treatment. You would be there about three months, although certain milestones have to be met so it's not a set in stone date. Hope, I'd really like to help you get help for your sake and for Lance's sake. He's already aware of what's going on. I would hate to see him follow in your path and think that substance use is a solution to a problem. He's going to be a teenager before too long and peer pressure is huge for someone like him. He needs a strong parent here at home that he can count on to help him through those struggles."

Neither of them had heard the door open, but they both looked up when a small voice said "Please, mom, let Ray help you." Lance stood there with tears rolling down his face. "Ray's really good at helping people. Please let him help you get better."

# Chapter 10

Hope had never realized just how much her drug use had affected her son. Though that was most likely because she was too far into her own addiction to see much of anything other than the fact that the drugs numbed the pain of having lost her husband at such a young age. She sat there and watched Lance with tears on his face and her own tears started to flow. When she was able to speak again, she said "Okay, I need to understand more about what all of this paperwork means and I want to talk to Sally and Steve too." She turned to Ray and asked, "Will I be able to see anyone while I'm there?"

"It's my understanding that there are different options." Ray began. He was being careful of just how much he said in front of Lance. "Some chose to use medications that are safe and effective to help get past the addiction, some chose to stay away from any further substances in their body. Those choices determine how quickly the symptoms from withdraw are over. I can't give you an exact timeframe because a lot depends on you and on how well things go with your treatment, but I can say that yes, visitors are allowed after a certain point in treatment. I will also promise you that I will facilitate any phone calls or visits between you and Lance that the program allows."

"Okay, I want to talk to my brother-in-law tonight when the diner is closed and then take it from there." Hope said.

Ray picked up his phone and called the diner when Sally answered he asked, "Would it be okay if Hope and I stopped by at closing time this evening, she would like to talk to you about becoming Lance's temporary guardian." She replied in the affirmative and Ray disconnected the call.

"It's practically dinner time anyway," Ray stated, "Why don't you two try to dry your eyes and I'll treat us all to dinner?"

Hope went to get cleaned up and changed into nicer clothes, although they still didn't fit well, and the sleeves were long. While she was gone, Lance asked "Do you think my mom will get better?"

"I think we're all going to do everything we can to help her do the best she can." Ray promised. He knew that he couldn't promise Lance that his mom would overcome her addiction that was fully reliant on how hard she was willing to work. "I think that the best thing all of us can do is support her and encourage her. I know you're going to miss her when she goes away, but we have to make sure she knows that we're going to be okay while she's gone so she doesn't have to worry about anything but getting better."

"I promise, I'll be good, and I'll do all my work and everything, so she doesn't have to worry about me." Lance said solemnly.

Hope walked out at the end of that statement, and she went to hug her son. "Oh, Lance, I know I haven't been here for you for a long time, I just didn't know how to do it right. But I'll always worry about you, you're my son, I've not been a good mom for a while, but I'll work on redeeming myself as a mother."

They all got into Ray's SUV for the drive to Sally's'. It was only a few blocks, but Ray wasn't sure if they would be out late. When that thought occurred to him, he said, "Hey Lance, we might be a while at Sally's, we have a lot to talk about, maybe we should go and feed Lucky real quick. We can't linger long, but that way he doesn't think we forgot him."

"Yeah, that's a good idea." Lance said. "That way my mom can meet my dog too."

Hope just raised her eyebrows and glanced at Ray across the front seat. He sort of shrugged, he hadn't thought about the fact that Lance was potentially adding a dog to the household and his mom may or may not be okay with that.

When they got to the park, Lance jumped out and waited for his mom to join him "See, mom." he said pointing. "Over there, that's Lucky, I'm trying to get him to be my dog. Ray's been helping me feed him and stuff, so he'll like me and learn to trust me."

Ray brought the dish of food around the vehicle and handed it to Lance. Lance took the bowl and slowly approached the dog, speaking the whole way. "Hey boy. I brought your dinner. I can't stay too long tonight; we've got to go talk about some important stuff. That's my mom over there. She won't be around for a while, but by the time she comes back, you'll be my dog for sure and you can be her dog too. She's a really nice mom. When my dad died, she was really sad and started doing somethings that made her sick, but she's going to go and get better."

Hope listened to every word her son uttered to the dog and watched him as he gave the dog food but respected it's fear and stepped back so the dog had space to eat. "Who are you and where did you come from Ray?" she asked.

"Well, um, I'm Ray Hawthorne. I used to live in LA, but I decided to travel around and see America. I take some pictures and send them back to magazines." Ray wasn't sure exactly what she was asking.

"Well, you definitely have the knack for helping people." Hope said.

Ray wasn't really sure what to say to that, so he just thanked her and then walked over to turn on the faucet so the water could start to run and cool down a little.

After Lucky had been fed and watered, they made their way back to the diner. Sally looked up when the bell rang and even though she had known they were supposed to be coming, she had a bit of a surprised look on her face. Ray wasn't sure if it was because they were early, or if she hadn't been sure Hope would actually follow through and show up. Others in the diner seemed surprised to see Hope walk in the door too. Ray just stood as tall as he could and guided Hope and Lance to a booth in the corner. He gave a look of disdain to anyone who seemed to be judging his group.

When they were seated, Sally brought over menus and said, "It's really good to see you Hope." She gave the other woman a genuine smile and then told them that the special tonight was sloppy joes with chips. She left them to look at the menus while she took food to another table.

It was obvious that Lance was so happy to have his mom with him. "I had white chicken chili here mom, it's really good. You should try it sometime. It didn't sound good, but it was." He barely took a breath before continuing "The sloppy joes are usually good too. I like to get a chocolate shake with mine. I really like it when the special is chicken tenders and macaroni and cheese."

Finally, Ray interjected, as much as he could understand the boy's excitement, he didn't want Hope to feel overwhelmed. "Hey, Lance, why don't you give your mom a minute to look at the menu and decide what she wants." He gave a smile and a wink so the boy would know he wasn't upset about anything he just wanted Lance to give his mom some space.

Lance didn't seem upset at all by Ray's correction and went back to looking at the menu as if he were taking time to study it too.

It was going to be a fine balance between Lance's excitement of having his mother seem active in his life for the first time in months and the boy going overboard with his happiness that it might push her a little too hard. Ray had glanced at Hope's face and while she was trying to smile to look happy to be here with her son, her eyes told a different story. She was stressed, she was nervous or anxious about what was to come and very likely at least a part of her was debating changing her mind about the whole thing and going back home to shut out the world and get high. He would never underestimate the amount of strength it was going to take for her to go through with this, if she could even do it. He would do everything he could to help her, but only she could actually make it happen.

Ray didn't have his camera with him, but he did have a pretty decent camera on his phone. He pulled it out and took a couple of pictures, some were taken before they knew he was taking them, and some were taken as they posed for the camera. Ray would figure out a way to get them printed or put on a device if Hope was allowed to have a digital photo frame of some kind. He had a strong feeling that Lance was going to be the only motivating factor that would potentially keep her working on her recovery.

The meal was pleasant, Ray could tell that Hope was having a hard time with it, whether it was being out in public, beginning symptoms of withdrawal or the fact that she didn't really know him, he wasn't sure. But she tried her best not to show her son that she was having any form of distress.

When the diner closed, Sally locked the door and called for her husband to come out front. They would worry about clean up later. She sat next to Ray and Steve pulled a chair up at the end of the table. Hope tucked her chin to her chest as if she were afraid to face what these people might say to her. Ray hoped that no one put her on the defensive, that would do no one any good.

Steve spoke first, "Hope, I know that we've had some struggles between us since Paul passed away, but I know that we need to put those aside to do what's best for Lance. I'm sorry for the part I played in us becoming distant. It's been so hard just looking at Lance, and I've not been a good uncle or brother-in-law because of it. But if you're willing to try, we are too. We'll do whatever is needed to make sure Lance is taken care of while you get help. And, when you get back, we'll be here to support you and help you too."

Hope looked up with tears in her eyes. "Thank you." she said softly.

Ray decided to treat this somewhat like a business meeting because there was a lot of important business to be dealt with. "So, what we have to discuss is the agreement for Lance being able to stay with his aunt and uncle for the time that his mom will be away." He was trying to not go into a lot of detail as to why Hope would be gone, they all knew the reason, they didn't need to discuss it.

He opened the file folder and pulled out the document. "I'd like for all of us to go over it here in private, but it does need two witnesses to the signatures. If we all agree we can fill it all out except for those and then I believe Maude would be glad to be a second witness, I of course can be the first."

He explained each section and what they had to agree to. There was a section where Hope could specify anything that she wanted to have enforced. If she wanted Lance to be taken to church, if he had any groups or clubs, she wanted him to be able to continue with and if he had any medications or treatments that needed to be followed up on. They marked that the guardianship was temporary but left the date as open ended with a note stating that it would last until Hope was finished with her treatment and able to take care of her son again.

When the document was filled out, they helped clean up what was left to do at the diner although Sally and Steve had been cleaning as they went knowing the important business that would be taking place after close. They drove to Maude's to finalize the signatures and Maude was happy to be a witness.

After the formalities were done, she told Hope, "I'm so glad you're getting help. I've come to really like your son while he's been here doing his homework. If there's ever anything that I can do, you just ask. I know we're not blood, but that doesn't mean we can't help one another when we need a hand up." She gave the other woman a brief hug. Hope was still awkward with a lot of it, Ray got the feeling that maybe she herself hadn't had the closest of families. It was obvious that she hadn't had any support from her family after her husband had died.

"The woman at the center made the recommendation that once you've decided to go into rehab, that you go immediately." Ray said. "It helps keep you from wanting to back out or maybe finding old ways to cope."

"I don't have any of my things." Hope objected, "I'd at least have to go and pack."

"I disagree." Ray said. He noticed that Maude and Sally were distracting Lance by talking about all of his schoolwork. "I would be willing to bet that you have some drugs at your home. I would also be willing to bet that this afternoon and evening has been stressful for you. If you go home, it will be far more tempting to take just one more, or to change your mind all together." He didn't say more, he just looked at her for a response.

"You're right, but I have to have clothes and toiletries." Hope stated.

"There just happens to be a twenty-four hour superstore on our way to San Bernadino. I will gladly buy whatever you need to feel comfortable going." Ray began. "If it's on the list of approved items you are allowed to have with you." He pulled the pamphlet out of his pocket and opened it to the page with the list.

"Why would you do all of this for me?" she asked confused.

"I don't know that I can explain that fully." Ray said. "I guess some would call it karma or a higher power or whatever, but I feel like I stopped in this town for a reason. Lance was one of the first people I saw when I got here and something about him made me want to know more. I feel like maybe I was brought here to help you find your way back so that Lance has a good home life."

"Do they let people just walk in in the middle of the night?" Hope asked.

“I’ll call ahead and if they don’t, we’ll find a hotel close by so we can go first thing in the morning.” Ray said. “I just want to help you stay away from your own demons. I know that the temptation right now must be huge, but for Lance’s sake, please lean on me and let me help you.”

Hope thought for several long minutes before saying “Okay.” She said her goodbyes and gave Lance lots of hugs and kisses and then they left the small town headed for rehab. In a way, Hope thought of this as the road to redemption for her as a mother.

They stopped at the shopping center and purchased a large duffel bag and a few outfits and the personal items that Hope would need. While she was picking out clothes and things, Ray went to the electronics department and purchased a photo device. It wouldn’t be able to do anything except receive photos that were either directly downloaded onto it or were sent to a specific email address. Hope wouldn’t be able to use it for anything other than receiving and storing photos that were sent to her. He also took time to call the number he had been given to reach the facility twenty-four hours a day. “Hello, my name is Ray Hawthorne, I met with Kelly the other day and we talked about a person that I was hoping to have enter your facility. She’s ready to begin treatment, but I wasn’t sure if we could come now or if there were certain times that were set aside for intake.” Ray would do whatever it took to babysit Hope until she was safely at the facility. He wasn’t going to take a chance on her finding a way to get more drugs into her system. The signs of withdraw were already getting fairly strong in his opinion, she was doing a lot of shaking and she was very fidgety. He was hoping that the act of shopping for new clothes would be distracting for her, but that didn’t mean that he didn’t keep glancing around to make sure he could still see her.

“Yes, sir, we do emergency intakes at anytime of the day or night.” the person stated. “Do you know when you might arrive so that we can prepare a room?”

“We should be there within an hour or so, we are just picking up some clothing and personal items and then we will be on our way.” Ray said.

“Okay, we’ll have a room ready when you get here. I’ll let Kelly know that you will be arriving.”

“Thank you.” Ray said and then hung up the phone. He walked to the women’s section to find Hope with a small cart of things. He noticed that she only had what he would consider three outfits really. “Hope, you’re going to need more clothing than that. I’m not sure how often you get to do laundry.”

“Well, I have jeans, I can wear jeans more than one day.” she explained.

“Okay, granted, but then you need at least more tops to go with them.” Ray argued.

“I don’t want you to have to spend a lot of money on me.” Hope said.

“Well, then we’ll consider it a loan for now and the terms have no end date.” Ray began. “You can pay me back whenever it works out for you.”

“Okay.” Hope agreed. She found a few more shirts and some more undergarments so that she would have plenty for whatever length of time she needed to go between loads of laundry.

When he was satisfied that she would have everything she needed and the list in the brochure was completely checked off, they paid and headed toward the facility.

“I called, and they do intake anytime, so they are getting your room ready right now.” Ray said. He was trying to keep Hope’s mind of off things, he could tell that she was desperately wanting to go back home and find her drugs right now. “I bought a photo device; I can upload some pictures of Lance to it and it has a way that I can send more directly to it while you’re gone. I promise to send you lots of pictures to help you remember your motivation for getting through this program and getting your life back on track.”

“Thank you.” Hope said. She was very quiet, but Ray kept talking about all sorts of things, He told her about some of the things Lance had done to win over the dog. He told her how well Lance was doing with his make-up work and how he was on track to move ahead with his class in the fall if he kept his focus and worked as hard as he had been. He talked about anything and everything just to try to keep her mind busy with anything other than her desire for drugs.

# Chapter 11

When they arrived at the facility, Ray grabbed the duffel bag. They had put all of their purchases inside of it in the parking lot of the store. When they walked in the front door, Kelly was waiting to greet them. Ray was impressed because he was sure that the staff could have handled the intake, but it was a nice touch that the director was there to meet the new resident.

"Hello, Hope, I'm Kelly. Welcome to Redemption House." Kelly held out her hand for a handshake. She could feel the tremors in Hope's hand.

Hope hadn't consciously realized that she had seen the name on the brochure, but apparently somewhere in her brain she had because she had been considering this her way to redeem herself. She knew her hands were trembling, but she was pretty sure the woman understood why.

"As a formality, we do have to check in your purse and duffel bag to be sure there aren't any substances being brought in." Kelly said.

"We stopped on our way here and bought everything that's in the duffel" Ray offered. "I helped her pack it while we were in the parking lot."

"Okay, we'll take your word for that" Kelly said. "But we still need to see the contents of your purse to be sure you aren't bringing in anything that is contraband."

"I'll tell you right now, there are drugs in my purse." Hope said. "I didn't even think about trying to get rid of them before we got here."

Ray was kind of astounded by that admission. "Hope, I'm really proud of you for not taking the opportunity to go to a bathroom or something and take some of that. It shows your determination to get better for you and for Lance." Ray praised.

Kelly helped Hope go through her purse and removed anything she wasn't allowed to keep. She had a small amount of cash that they told her they could lock in a safe in an envelope with her name on it or she could have Ray take it home for her. She opted for Ray to take it.

"I did buy her one of those digital photo frames." Ray began. "I uploaded several photos to it already, but will she be able to have it on a network where I can send her more?"

"Is it just a photo box and can't do anything else on the Internet?" Kelly asked.

"It is."

"Then that's fine, we want you to be able to have photos of your family and friends, it's always a good reminder of why you want to get better." Kelly said.

"Will I be able to have visitors, can my son come and see me?" Hope asked.

"He can, but not right away." Kelly explained. "Anyone, but most especially a child doesn't really understand some of the signs of withdraw that addicts go through and I'm sure you only want him to see you at your best. When you get to that stage, we'll have you call Ray and set up a time for a visit."

Kelly showed them the room that Hope was being assigned and explained that the doors were on a sensor, she wasn't locked in, but if she did open the door, it would be monitored. She had her own bathroom so other than meals and group or individual therapy, she didn't need to leave her room until she felt ready to socialize with others.

She had a closet and a dresser, so she set about unpacking her things. Ray was sure that was at least in part to help with the fidgeting and restlessness of wanting to take drugs but not having them available anymore. She plugged the photo device in and scrolled through to a picture Ray had taken at the diner a few hours before. She and Lance were looking at each other and

Lance had a huge grin on his face. That was how she wanted to picture him, and she was hoping she could put that smile there a lot more in the future.

While she was settling her belongings, Kelly had been asking questions to fill out the intake paperwork. "Now, I have to ask" Kelly began. "We have medications that will help with the withdraw symptoms, some people want them, some people don't, some only want them administered if the person gets to the point of extreme or dangerous behavior. Which would you prefer, Hope?"

Hope looked to Ray as if she wasn't sure what she wanted so he said. "It's up to you, Hope. Personally, I've always felt that scientist make medications for a reason and using them isn't bad as long as they aren't something that a person can get addicted to." He sort of shrugged because his feelings didn't necessarily have to line up with hers.

"They aren't going to get me hooked on something else?" She asked Kelly.

"Nope, there's nothing addictive in them and we only give a dose that will help minimize things, it won't give you a feeling to counter the withdraw, but it will lessen what is happening in your body and brain."

"Then I think I'd like to try them." Hope said.

"Good, it generally helps people get through stage one faster and easier, but we will never force anyone to take them. That's a big part of how we work, we won't force you to get off of drugs, you are free to leave at anytime if this isn't working for you, but we will provide all of the tools necessary for you to help yourself get better." Kelly pushed some buttons on a device in her pocket and a few minutes later, a woman in scrubs came in with a small medicine cup and a bottle of water.

Hope took the medication and kept the bottle of water, taking sips frequently. Ray couldn't imagine what she was going through, but he knew it must have been a form of torment. Hopefully the medication would kick in fast, and she would be able to at least get some rest.

When they were finished with the business aspects, Kelly excused herself so that they could say their goodbyes and told Ray she would meet him downstairs to show him out.

“I’m really proud of you Hope, and I know that everyone back home is too, especially Lance. You keep your focus and do what needs to be done and you’ll be better in no time.” Ray said and he gave her a one arm hug.

“Thank you for everything, Ray.” Hope said. “I still don’t really understand why you’re doing all this, but I’m grateful that you are.”

“Just get better and come home to be a good mom for Lance, I’ll consider that paying it forward for what I’m doing for you now.” Ray said. He gave her one last nod of encouragement and made his way back downstairs to meet with Kelly.

“I believe her insurance will cover this, but I would need a document signed that anything not covered will be paid for, it’s also there in case any incidentals come up.” Kelly said. “I’m not sure if you’re willing to sign that though, I don’t really know what your connection to her is.”

“I’m just a friend, but I’ll sign it.” Ray said. “And please call me if she needs anything. I’ll get it here as soon as I can. I want this to be successful for her and for her son.”

Ray signed the document and headed to his car. He called Sally to let her know that Hope was safely signed into the facility, and he was heading back to town. Lance had apparently had a long and full day because he was already sleeping in the room he had been given at his uncle and aunt’s house.

Ray made the drive back to Maude’s house and was surprised to find Maude still up. It was well past midnight. “You didn’t have to wait up.” he told the older woman. He locked the door behind him.

“Oh, I know, but I worry about those that I consider family and I wanted to make sure you got in safe.” Maude said. “But now, it’s time for bed.” She stood up and turned off the light by her chair. Just before heading down the hall, she turned and said, “This is a good thing you’re doing Ray, a real good thing.” She turned and walked to her room.

He went upstairs and his head barely hit his pillow before he was out like a light. He slept deeply, a sense of hope for the future settled in around him.

Ray wasn't sure how things would go in the future as far as he and Lance meeting in the mornings to feed the dog and hang out for a while before lunch and homework. Technically, Sally was now responsible for Lance, and she may have different plans in mind for how she wanted the boy's days to go. He headed to the park anyway because Lance or no Lance, the dog would be looking for food and Ray didn't want it reverting back to its old habit of relying on dumpsters and whatever scraps it might find while scrounging.

Lance was sitting in his usual spot near the edge of the park and Lucky was not far away. Ray got the dish and the food ready and walked over to hand it to Lance. The boy put it down for the dog and then he said, "Aunt Sally said that mom got there okay, is she really okay?"

"She is, Lance," Ray said. "She has a nice room, and I got her a photo box and filled it with pictures of you and some of you and her together yesterday. We can even take more and email them to her although we shouldn't do that like every day or whatever, it will get filled up too fast, but we can maybe take some and every week pick a few favorites to send her and the rest she can see when she gets home. They're going to help her get better Lance and then when she comes home it will be up to all of us to help her stay on track."

"I won't do anything bad to make her upset" Lance said. "I promise."

"It's not so much that Lance, you don't have to be any different than you already are. But she will probably have to go once a week to a meeting somewhere, and we need to help her do that. If you see anything that makes you think she's taking drugs again, tell an adult, especially your aunt or uncle." That reminded Ray that someone needed to go to Hope's house and do a thorough cleaning to make sure any stash of drugs was found and disposed of properly. The last thing they needed was for Hope to come home clean and then stumble on some drugs and be tempted to go back down that road. He had the key to her house because she had given him most of the contents of her purse, but he wouldn't go there without talking to Sally to be sure that was how she wanted it handled.

Lance played fetch with Lucky, and they gave him some cool water to drink. Then the boy asked Ray if they could bat some balls and Ray agreed although he suggested they do that at the schoolyard so that Lucky didn't get confused by what was going on with the ball.

When it was time for lunch, they went to Sally's as usual and sat in a booth. Ray mentioned to Sally that he had the key and would be glad to do whatever she felt was best to clean the house for Hope's return. He didn't spell it out fully, but he did say that it was probably a good idea to make sure that there wasn't food that would spoil or anything else that Hope wouldn't want to have in the house when she came home from rehab. Sally agreed with his assessment and said she was fine with him stopping by to look things over but if he needed any help with the cleaning to let her know.

He also made sure that Sally was okay with the things he and Lance usually did during the day. If she wanted to take over on helping with the schoolwork or wanted him home by a certain time, Ray wanted to make sure he followed her rules. Sally had told him in all honesty that while they were glad that Hope had gone to get help, they hadn't been planning for becoming guardians so quickly and while they were happy to adjust their schedule and even hire extra help at the diner, they would need a few days at least to do so. If Ray wanted to continue to help with all the things he had already been doing, they would gladly accept.

"You know, Lance doesn't really have clothes or his things." Sally said, "maybe sometime today you can go over there and help him pack his stuff for staying at our house for a while. It might give you a chance to look around and see if there's going to be anything that needs cleaning."

Ray knew she was talking about the drugs that may be there and while the time it took Lance to pack wasn't a lot of time for Ray to dig around, it would give him a few minutes at least and the boy did need his belongings. He was going to be staying with his aunt for a while. "That's a good idea, Lance does need his stuff and maybe I can take a quick look around and see if there's stuff that's not going to last. Then I have an idea of what will need to be done."

When they finished their lunch, they went to Lance's house. As they walked up the sidewalk, a woman from next door stepped out and said, "Excuse me, you're Ray right?"

Ray turned to her and said, "I am, I remember seeing you at the picnic, but I'm afraid I didn't get your name."

"Oh, I'm Barbara, Barbara Johnson." she said. "I just wanted to let you know that a man stopped by here earlier. He was pounding on the door something fierce. He was hollering for Hope. I told him she wasn't home, and I wasn't sure she would be back for a while. He didn't seem to like that answer much, but he said he would be back and then he left. I just thought you should know that someone is looking for her."

Ray had a pretty good idea who that someone would be, very likely her dealer either hoping to make a new sale or collect on a delivery that was made previously depending on whether or not Hope had been buying from him long enough that he felt comfortable extending her a 'line of credit'. Either way, the man would need to be dealt with and not when Lance was around either. Ray was going to have to rely heavily on Maude if she was willing to help. He thought of the perfect plan to take care of the lowlife too. He'd just have to shoot him, oh not with a gun, but if he could get enough pictures of the man and his vehicle, it would be given to law enforcement for them to pursue. He pulled a card out of his wallet and said, "This is an old business card from when I was working in LA, but the cellphone number is still accurate, if you see him again, would you mind giving me a call."

"No, of course not, I'd be happy to." Barbara said taking the card.

"I appreciate it." Ray said. He and Lance went in the house, and he helped the boy find a couple of boxes to pack his things in. He took time to look around a little but didn't really want to do too much digging with Lance there. Besides, it sounded like he was going to be coming back soon to throw out the trash, both the actual food that would spoil and the trash that was going to try to keep Hope in her addiction.

When the things were packed, they dropped them off at Sally and Steve's house, it was the first time Ray had been there other than walking by on their tour, so Lance showed him which room was his. It was a decent sized family home and it made Ray wonder if they had any plans to have children of their own someday.

"Well, we better get started on your homework for today, we can't slack off if you want to move on to the next grade." Ray said.

When they got to Maude's she already had the table set up ready for Lance to get to work. He sat down and Maude immediately sat with him to help. Ray didn't say anything, it would be a good thing that Lance was making connections with other people. As much as Ray knew he was staying until Hope was home and things were on track for her and Lance, he still had his dream of traveling. He stayed close by so that Lance knew he had the added support, but he let them work together without interruption.

They were on the porch enjoying their mid study break when Ray's phone rang. He didn't recognize the number, but he picked it up. A woman on the other end said, "That man just pulled up." He realized it was Barbara so he told her he would be right there. He told Maude and Lance that he had something he needed to take care of but they should go ahead and finish the schoolwork if he wasn't back.

It was really only a few blocks to walk, but he wanted to get there quickly so he took his SUV. He parked around the corner and got out his camera, as he walked up, he started snapping photos of the man's vehicle, license plate and the man himself. When he was sure he at least had enough to identify the car, he spoke up "Can I help you?"

"No, I'm just here looking for my friend Hope." he said.

Now that the man was turned towards him, Ray began snapping more pictures of his face.

"Hey, what are you doing?" he yelled.

"Taking photos, you see, I have pictures of your car and the plate and now I have pictures of your face." Ray began. "If anyone comes here trying to sell to Hope again, I'm turning this whole memory card over to the police. I don't even care if it's you, so you better start spreading the word. This house, this neighborhood and especially Hope are off limits. Anyone shows up here again, I'm turning you in to the cops, so you better make sure the word spreads fast."

"She owes me money man" he was belligerent, "I'm not walking away without my money."

"How much?" Ray spat out.

"Two hundred man."

Ray pulled out his wallet and threw two one hundred dollar bills at the man. "Now, get out of here and never come back."

The man scrambled to pick up the money and then got in his car and sped away.

Ray didn't realize it, but several people were on their porches watching the whole interaction. Barbara began clapping and the others joined in. Ray held up his hands and said, "I don't deserve applause, but I'd appreciate it if you'd help keep an eye on this house while Hope is gone and maybe even after she gets back if you see guys like that show up again."

Several of them vocalized their agreement to do so and Ray thanked them before walking back to his SUV. He drove back to Maude's and took a few minutes to regain his composure before going inside to check on Lance. He didn't want the boy to sense his anger and frustration at having to deal with that man, but he would do it again if he needed to. He wasn't going to make it easy for anyone to attempt to get Hope hooked on drugs again.

When he walked in, they both looked up from the table. "Hey, how's it going?" he said trying to sound like what he had just done was no big deal at all.

"It's going good." Maude said. "Lance is going to need a new subject to work on tomorrow. He's almost done with social studies."

"That's great, Lance!" Ray praised. "You're doing so good. Your mom will be so proud when she gets home."

Lance was beaming from ear to ear at the praise. "Can we call Mrs. Cooper and see if we can get the next subject tomorrow?"

"Sure, I'll call her right now." Ray said. "You finish up so we can have time to have a cookie before we go feed Lucky."

The rest of the week went smoothly, Ray didn't hear from Barbara, so he was assuming that the dealer had gotten the message at least for now. He had no doubt that he might try again when he heard that Hope was back in town. They just had to believe that she would come home strong enough to tell him to leave on her own.

After he had gotten Lance started on the next subject, which was English, he told Lance that he was going to take one afternoon and go and clean out the refrigerator and things at the house so that things didn't get smelly before Hope got back. He emptied the refrigerator and cupboards of anything that would go out of date and did a thorough sweep of most of the house. He didn't feel right cleaning Hope's bedroom though because of her personal things. He would have to see if Sally was willing to help with that. He had found some paraphernalia, but no actual drugs. He was seeing that as a good thing because it most likely meant that Hope had kept them out of the area of the house Lance would be most likely to spend time in.

# Chapter 12

The following Saturday morning, Ray had told Lance that he may need to come to Maude's to wait for a bit before going to feed Lucky. He had something else he needed to take care of. Maude was in the kitchen finishing the dishes from breakfast when Ray called out to her to come into the dining room.

"What is it, Ray?" she asked coming into the room. Ray stepped to the side so that she could see what he had set up on the table. There she saw a tablet with her son and one of her grandkids both waving at her. She waved back as tears started to form in her eyes.

"Hi mom." Bill junior said into the camera.

"Hi gramma." The small child echoed.

"Oh, my." Maude said sitting in the chair in front of the tablet. "Bill, Katie, I can't believe it's really you."

"It's us mom." Bill assured. "I've got the first call, when we finish, I'll text Betsy and she'll call you and then Nick is last. But all of us promise we will set a time at least once a week for a video call so you can see us, and the grandkids can all see you too. I don't know why none of us ever thought of doing this before, but we're all really glad that Ray came up with the idea and helped you get it set up on your end."

She turned to thank Ray, but he was already gone, leaving her privacy to talk to her family as long as she desired.

Ray and Lance made their way down to the park to feed Lucky. The dog was anxiously waiting for them. Every time they came, he was less and less timid. In fact, he sat wagging his tail when he saw Lance approaching with the dish of food. He stood up and took a few steps forward and met Lance part way. When Lance sat down the bowl, Lucky eagerly dug into the food. He didn't even worry about keeping an eye on Lance for any sudden movement. Ray still stayed back several feet. Once the dog was completely secure with Lance, it would be more likely to let the boy introduce it to others that he could trust.

After the dog had been fed and watered, Ray asked, "It's Saturday, it's up to you if you want to get any homework in today. We really don't need to if you don't want to. We're on track for finishing in plenty of time before school starts in a few weeks."

"I'd like to go for a drive today if we can." Lance said.

"Where do you want to go?" Ray asked. He knew the boy probably hadn't ever left the town much at all other than to go to the slightly larger town nearby for pizza or other shopping.

Lance looked at his feet kicking at the dirt and said, "I want to see where my mom is."

Ray was kind of surprised at that request. "I'm sorry, Lance," he began. "You can't see your mom yet; she has some things to work on before she can have visitors."

"I know." Lance admitted. "I just want to see where she is so that I know she's safe."

Ray could understand that request and if the place looked institutional, he would try to discourage the boy from seeing it for as long as he could, but it wasn't. He didn't see a problem with taking Lance past the place, but he wasn't going to make a call like that without his guardian's approval. "Well, I'll have to check with your aunt and uncle, I don't have permission to take you that far away unless they say it's okay. We'll have to go talk to them."

"Okay!" The boy said with excitement running towards Ray's SUV.

They drove to the diner and Lance was just as excited to get out of the vehicle and run inside to talk to his aunt. Ray cautioned him to slow down because there might be people coming or going from the diner. Lance slowed his speed slightly, but not his excitement at asking his aunt if Ray could take him for a ride.

When he told her where he wanted to go, she just looked up at Ray who was several steps behind. Ray just shrugged and said, "It was totally his idea. He came up with it on his own. I did explain to him that he won't be able to see his mom though."

"I know." Lance said. "I just want to see where she is. It's not a big scary place, is it? I'd hate for her to be alone in a big scary place."

"Actually, it's a really big house." Ray stated.

"Can I please go see it Aunt Sally." Lance pleaded. "I promise I won't get out of the car, and I will behave and mind whatever Ray tells me to do."

"How long will it take?" she asked looking at Ray.

"Most of the rest of the day to get there and back. We'll probably grab lunch somewhere on the way up." Ray explained. "If it's okay, we might stop for pizza on the way back."

Steve had stepped up to the order window to see what was going on. He and Sally shared a look and a shrug and then he went back to his work. Sally turned to Lance and said, "Okay, but you stay in the car unless Ray tells you it's time to get out. You mind him, no matter what he says to do."

"I will, thanks Aunt Sally!" He wrapped his arms around her waist and gave her a hug. He ran into the kitchen and said, "Thanks Uncle Steve!" He eagerly ran to the door, dodging customers along the way. He hopped into Ray's SUV like he was going on the most exciting journey of his life.

After they were out of the small town a few miles, Lance asked, "That man Mrs. Johnson was talking about is the man who gave drugs to my mom wasn't he?"

"I'm pretty sure he was." Ray said. "Have you ever seen him?"

“I don’t know, I think so, maybe.” Lance said. “I remember seeing a man walk out of our house one day when I was going home. He got into a green car and drove away.”

“That’s him.” Ray said. “If you ever see him around your house or around town again, you let me know okay. You don’t try to talk to him or anything, but you let me know he was there.”

“Okay.” the boy agreed.

“I talked to him and told him to stay away, but if he doesn’t, I want to know about it, and I’ll tell the police.” Ray promised.

Lance was quiet until they stopped at a fast food place for their lunch. Even then, he seemed reserved, he usually wasn’t one to stay quiet for long. Ray wondered if he was regretting wanting to go see where his mom was if he couldn’t go inside to see her. “Hey, you’re kind of quiet, are you sure you want to make the ride all the way up there if you’re not going to be able to see your mom?”

“Yeah, I need to know where she is.” Lance said solemnly.

They ate their food and got back on the road, Lance was still too quiet in Ray’s opinion, but he supposed the kid had a lot on his mind lately. As they got close to the large house, Ray slowed down and eventually came to a stop on the road where there was a good view of the building. “That’s the place, Lance. Your mom is staying there.”

Lance looked in disbelief, it looked like a big house, there were flowers in the yard and trees and the greenest grass he had ever seen. He had never seen a house as huge as this one was. Tears started to roll down his face.

Dang, Ray hadn’t expected the kid to cry. He knew it probably wouldn’t be easy for him, but he hadn’t expected him to cry. “Hey, Lance, it’s okay. They’re taking really good care of your mom, I promise. It won’t be too many more days before you can see her. I promise just as soon as they say she’s ready, we’ll come up here and visit.” He was scrambling for words to say to comfort the kid.

“I’m not crying because I’m sad,” Lance began. “I thought she would have to be in a big ugly place that looked like a hospital or a prison, but she’s at a really nice place."

Ray wondered if the boy was afraid that she would like it there and not want to come home. "Yeah, it's a nice place, but she'll only stay here however long it takes for her to get better. I promise she wants to come home."

"No, I don't mean that." Lance said trying to dry his eyes. "I'm just happy that you found her a nice place and they're going to help her get better. I don't know how to say thank you for everything you've done for all of us. I feel kind of like you're an angel or something."

"I'm not an angel, Lance, I just, I don't know, I've always liked helping people and I kind of feel like if God or karma or whatever puts me in a place where I can help someone, I should do it." Ray explained. "I had things happen in my life and there were people that always came along and helped me out. See, my dad didn't die like yours but he left my mom and me. For a long time, I really hated him for that and that hate made me really turn bitter inside. I never talked to my dad again. He did die, a couple of years ago, and I realized that having hate didn't do me any good. I have a half brother out there somewhere that I've never met because I was so angry and hateful. About a year ago, when I decided I was going to retire as soon as I could, I decided that I was going to travel and meet people and I was going to do my best to spread love and kindness to anyone I met."

"Are you ever going to find your brother?" Lance asked. "I sure wish I had a brother."

"I've been thinking about it, more and more lately." Ray said. "I'm not sure yet, but maybe."

Lance just nodded and took another long look at the house where his mother was. Finally, he asked, "Does she have her own room?"

"She does. It's a nice room, she has a bed and a small loveseat to sit on. She has a table where she can write or study the things they are helping her with."

"And you got her clothes and stuff, right?" Lance asked.

"We stopped at a store on our way here and bought her enough clothes and things for however long she has to stay." Ray assured. "She can do laundry here when she needs to." He wanted the boy to feel secure in the fact that his mom had everything to be comfortable.

"What does she do all day?" Lance asked.

"Well, at first, she does a lot of talking to people that know how to help her. Once she's settled, she gets to help with chores, like maybe work in the kitchen or help with the laundry or cleaning." Ray explained.

"I hope she gets to work in the kitchen." Lance said happily, "She's a really good cook, well she was before anyway." The end part was said with some sorrow, obviously she had changed in a lot of ways since Lance's dad died.

"Well, hopefully when she gets home, she'll be back to doing the things that she always loved and she won't be so sad about your dad anymore." Ray said. "I'm sure she'll always miss him, but these people are going to help her find ways to handle that sadness without using drugs to help her feel better."

"Yeah, that would be good." Lance said. "I can't wait until she's better."

"Me too, Lance, me too." Ray agreed.

After Lance had spent several more minutes looking at the big house, Ray asked, "Are you ready to go grab some pizza and then head home so we can make sure Lucky gets his dinner?"

"Yeah, I'm ready." Lance said. After Ray had started driving, Lance added, "Thanks for brining me so that I know my mom isn't in a scary place."

"It's no problem, Lance." Ray said. "I just want things to work out good for your mom and you."

They drove back towards Thousand Palms but stopped at Lance's favorite pizza place. Ray let him order anything he wanted on the pizza, which basically meant lots of pepperoni and lots of cheese. He let Lance get a small, decaffeinated soda, he hoped that one wasn't off limits. He kind of felt like the kid deserved something fun as a treat, going and sitting outside of your mom's rehab facility couldn't be a great experience for a kid.

When they got back to town, they went directly to the park to check on Lucky. The dog immediately came out of its hiding spot when it saw that it was Lance and not a stranger. By the time the dog was fed and watered, it was getting a little late and almost time for the diner to close. Ray wasn't sure if Lance now had a curfew or not, so he told the boy they should probably go check in with Sally and Steve.

When they arrived at the diner, Lance was excited to get inside and tell his aunt "You should see the place that Ray took my mom. It's so nice, I was afraid it would be some big scary place, but it's like a house, only it's huge. It has flowers and pretty trees in the yard, my mom must be so happy there."

Sally smiled and gave Ray a small nod of thanks. "It sounds great, we'll all have to go visit when your mom's ready for that." Sally said. "Seems like you had a pretty good day."

"We did, we had the best day." Lance exclaimed. "Can I get a chocolate milk?"

"Sure, go ahead and grab a glass," Sally said. "You know where it is."

"Well, I should head back to Maude's, but I did want to ask you if you have a specific curfew, you want Lance in by. I don't want to be breaking any of your rules." Ray said.

"Not really now but after school starts, we will have one set." Sally said. "Right now, it's all so new we're sorting out how to work all of this. When it was just the two of us, it wasn't hard to just run this place by ourselves. We don't get so much business that the two of us can't handle it and if we need a few days off, we just close. The logistics of this are different and we'll have to figure out how we're going to make family time."

"When I took Lance to your place, it made me wonder if you had ever considered having a family, your house is big enough for one." Ray said.

"We always talked about it," Sally said glancing toward the kitchen. "But we got so busy running this place that it got put on the back burner so to speak. I think it was always a touchy subject for Steve. Their mom wasn't a great mom. Their dad died when they were young and well, their mom never abused them or anything, but she always seemed to have more time for the boyfriend of the moment than for her kids. Steve ended up doing a lot of the parenting. I think it kind of put him in a place where he didn't want to have kids right away because he finally got to not be responsible for others. But he always said he wanted them someday. It's just that someday hasn't come yet."

Ray thought that Sally looked like she wished 'someday' was coming soon. "Well, maybe having Lance around will help him see that kids can be great."

"Maybe" Sally just nodded sadly but she looked like she wasn't at all sure that would happen.

Ray said his goodbyes, promised to meet Lance to feed Lucky in the morning and made his way to Maude's house. When he walked in, the entire house smelled amazing. It smelled a lot like pecan pie.

"Oh, Ray! You're home." Maude exclaimed "Thank you so much for what you did for me today. I got to spend hours with my babies. I made you some pie to thank you for the way you blessed me. I know you said it's one of your favorites."

"You don't have to thank me, Maude." Ray said. "And you really didn't need to bake a pie just for me."

"Oh, nonsense." Maude said brushing away his statement. "You've given this old woman so much joy since you came here. You gave me a way to see my grandbabies and my children. You gave me the opportunity to spend time with Lance and be a sort of surrogate grandma to him. I have so many things to thank you for, Ray. A pie was just a small token of all of the appreciation I have for you."

"Well, it's been my pleasure, Maude." Ray said. "But I won't turn down a pecan pie."

They sat and enjoyed their pie while Maude told him all about what was new in the lives of her family.

# Chapter 13

On Sunday, after Ray and Lance had spent the morning with Lucky and playing both catch and fetch, they went to the diner for lunch. Ray noticed two signs on the door. One was a help wanted sign, the other was a sign informing patrons that the hours would be changing, and the diner would now be closed on Sundays starting the following week. When Sally came to the table to see if they wanted menus, Ray said, “I see the signs on the door.”

“We had a long talk last night and realized that as guardians to Lance, we owe him more of our time and attention. Right now, I know he spends a lot of time with you, and we don’t intend to change that, but he should have us around more too. We always ran the place alone because we were trying to build a nest egg and not paying help made that grow faster, but at some point the egg is bigger than you will really need in life and you spent the whole time building and no time enjoying it.”

“That sounds like a really solid plan.” Ray stated.

“So, when we get a few people trained, we can at least take turns not being here and we can make Sundays a family day.” Sally said. “Besides, I haven’t even had a chance to meet this dog I keep hearing about.” She added smiling at Lance.

“He’s a really great dog, Aunt Sally.” Lance exclaimed. “His name is Lucky, and he plays fetch really good. I can’t wait till you get to meet him.”

Sally smiled and said she would be back to get their orders in a few minutes, another customer had walked in.

Over the next week, things went as usual for the most part, although Ray had noticed a couple of new faces at the diner. Apparently, the help wanted sign was doing its job and people were getting trained. A new sign had appeared in the window showing the new hours with Sunday's being closed.

On Sunday, when Ray got to the park to meet Lance, he wasn't there yet, so Ray started getting the food ready. He had no problem with taking care of the dog if Lance was going to be having a family day with his aunt and uncle. But before he had the food in the bowl, their sedan pulled up and Lance hopped out of the car to help.

Lance took the bowl from Ray and started explaining the process to his aunt. "See, we take it to him slow, so he knows we're not trying to do anything bad. When we first started, I had to set it down and back way off, but now he trusts me, and I can set it down pretty close."

As he continued to explain things to his aunt, Ray gestured for Steve to sit with him at a picnic table. "He's a really great kid, despite the tough things that happened in his life."

"Yeah, I'm just starting to realize that." Steve said. "I've missed out on a lot of it I guess."

Ray didn't want to go into the reasons that the uncle had struggled, he wanted the man to see the positive of the now. "Well, from what I hear you're at least partially responsible for the way Lance turned out."

"I don't see how." the man stated.

"Well, Sally told me that you lost your dad at a young age too, so you stepped up and helped raise your siblings. I think Lance's dad learned how to be a good dad by watching your example. And in turn, Lance is a pretty responsible kid because his dad taught him right. And now, you're stepping up to make sure he's got a place to be while his mom is in rehab. You may not think you're a dad, but I assure you, what you've done as a father figure has built a legacy that Lance will remember for life."

Steve didn't say anything more about that for a while, but Ray could tell he was thinking about it. Finally, he said "So, it looks like we're going to be taking in a dog soon too."

Ray looked over and Sally was on the ground with Lance attempting to make friends with Lucky. "Looks like it."

They invited Ray to their house for dinner. It would give them a chance to get to know each other and discuss how things would be going in the future while Lance was temporarily staying with them. Ray wanted to be sure he respected any rules they had put in place. He realized that Hope hadn't really had any, but that might not be the case anymore. If they wanted a curfew in place, or they wanted to take over with his teacher, Ray would step back and just support them in whatever way they wanted him to. If Hope got better, the four of them would need to work together to be a support system better than they had been in the past. If she didn't get better, things might have to get taken care of by the court system and that would be difficult for everyone involved. Ray wanted to be supportive of whatever was best for Lance for the long term. He really prayed that Hope would get her life back on track and be a good mom to her son and become a part of this small town, she would have so much love and support if she would just reach out and take it.

It was decided that Lance's curfew didn't really need to change until school started, unless it got to be worrisome that he was out really late. He could still ride in Ray's SUV if it was in town, but they wanted to discuss any drives out of town. All in all, not much in Lance's life changed really for now. He was welcome to come to the diner for help with his schoolwork if Ray or Maude wasn't able to do it because with the extra help, Sally might be able to take a few minutes to help him although they all still agreed that the diner would probably be much more distracting than the table at Maude's.

Ray contacted the rehab facility to check on Hope's progress. He was happy to find that Hope was doing well, really well. In fact, if her next week continued in the same manner, she would be allowed visitors the following week. They cautioned Ray not to tell Lance though because there was always a chance of a setback, and the boy would not likely handle that well. He would tell Sally when he had a moment alone with her. But for now, he wanted Lance to know that his mom was okay. "Hey, Lance, I just talked to the place where your mom is and they said she's doing really good. If she keeps making progress, she might get to have visitors before too long."

"Yay!" Lance yelled with glee. "When I get to see her, can I take her something nice, like flowers or something. I want her to have something pretty in her room."

"I'll check to be sure, but I think that's okay." Ray said. "But we don't know when we get to go yet."

"I know, I just thought about it and wanted to ask before I forget." Lance explained.

While Lance was busy playing with his uncle and the new set of Legos his uncle had picked up for him, Ray took the opportunity to talk to Sally. "The facility said that as long as Hope does okay this week, she might be able to see Lance next weekend. I'm not going to say anything until we know for sure, but I wanted you to be prepared."

"Okay." Sally said. "I think for the first time it should just be you and Lance. I am sure we will visit her, but I think she may need some time to try to explain to Lance just what happened for her."

"I think that's a good idea." Ray agreed. "I was also wondering, I went to the house and cleaned up any food that might spoil or go out of date. I took out the trash, and I did find a few things, but not much. I'm guessing most of it would be in Hope's bedroom and I just wasn't comfortable going through her personal items, I'm basically a stranger."

"I'll take care of it, in fact, I'll get a group of ladies together and we'll go do a thorough cleaning of everything. I'll do most of the bedroom myself, but we'll do the windows and everything so when Hope comes home it's all fresh and nice for her." Sally said.

"That sounds like a really great idea." Ray said.

"Oh, and Ray." Sally began, "You may be new to town and a stranger to some, but you've done more for several people in this town than people who have lived here for years have."

Ray just gave a slight bow of his head at her statement.

Lance worked extra hard the following week and completed all but a few assignments. He had explained that he wanted it all done so that if they called and said he could go see his mom nothing would make him not be able to go. School was less than a month away and he didn't want anything to mess up his being able to move up but he also didn't want to miss going to see his mom as often as possible once it was okay.

Ray got the call Friday night, that he could bring Lance the following morning. Hope had requested that it just be the two of them for the first visit. Ray wasn't sure why she was hesitant to see Sally or Steve, but he figured this was all a process and she had to deal with it in the manner that worked best for her. They had duties at the diner anyway even with the new hired help, Saturdays were a pretty busy day. He did call the diner and tell Sally, just to be sure they were okay with him taking Lance. They were, but they wanted to tell him when they all got home that night, so, Ray kept his secret until morning.

When Ray arrived at the park the next morning, Lance as waiting for him. He seemed like he was both anxious and nervous. He was dressed in clothes that looked like he had taken care with choosing the things that looked the best. "You look nice today, Lance." Ray said as he approached the boy and his dog.

"Thanks, I wanted to wear my best stuff cause I want to look good for my mom." Lance said.

"That's really nice, but I bet she's just so happy to see you that you could wear anything." Ray said.

"You really think she'll be happy to see me?" Lance asked.

"Oh, I'm sure of it." Ray replied.

"For a long time, it didn't feel like she was really happy to have me come home. That's why I stayed out a lot." Lance began. "At first, she was sad all the time. It made me even more sad because I could never make her happy. She cried a lot and slept a lot." He paused and then added, "Then she stopped sleeping she didn't sleep much at all, but she acted weird. I didn't like being around her because I didn't know if I was going to make her mad or happy. I didn't know if she was going to be singing or crying." He had his face turned down to the ground as if admitting all of that had been a difficult task. He didn't want to speak ill of his mother.

"Lance." Ray said and waited until the boy looked him in the eye. "That wasn't your mom, not really, it was the drugs. The sad part, yeah, that was normal, but when she changed that was probably when she started using the drugs. And she didn't mean to not be a good mom, she just wasn't sure how with all of what her mind was going through."

"I know." Lance said timidly.

"Well, we better get Lucky fed so we can get going." Ray said trying to sound upbeat. "I bet your mom is so anxious to see you."

On their way up to the facility, they stopped at a small store and picked up some flowers for Hope. Lance had his own money to pay for them. He said he and his aunt had worked out a plan for him to be able to get an allowance for doing certain things like keeping his room clean and making his bed. He seemed really proud that he had earned the money. Ray had no doubt that had been at least partially instilled in hm by his father.

Hope was waiting in the main foyer to greet them. Ray immediately noticed the changes in the woman. She was already starting to look like she was at a more healthy weight, her hair was shiny and wavy rather than straight and almost stringy. But her eyes were what told most of the story. Her eyes didn't look haunted anymore, they looked like she was alive and ready to face her new life. Oh, she still had some work to do, but there was a noticeable change in her demeanor and appearance. She invited them to go out onto the large patio with her. There were several seating areas, she chose one that was mostly in the shade. She sat on a small love seat and motioned for Lance to sit with her. Ray sat in one of the chairs facing them. She wrapped one arm around her son and gave him a one arm hug. "It's so good to see you, Lance." She had some moisture in her eyes. Ray had a feeling those were a mixture of happiness at seeing her son and sorrow at all the time she had lost.

"I brought you flowers." Lance began he handed her the flowers. "I earned my own money to pay for them too. Aunt Sally is giving me an allowance for keeping my room clean and stuff."

"They're beautiful, Lance." Hope said taking them and giving them a smell before laying them on the table in front of her. "We'll take them up to my room in a bit. I wanted to have a little talk first."

"Okay." Lance said.

"First, I'm so proud of you for being such a smart boy. Ray told me you're almost caught up with all of the schoolwork. I'm proud of you for what you are doing to help around the house at Sally and Steve's" Hope began. "I also want you to know that I'm so sorry I've made such a mess of things since your daddy died. I was just so sad that I could only think about myself. As a mom, I should have done much better. I knew you were feeling bad too, but I was just selfish I guess, and I couldn't get past that. I want you to know that I'm working really hard to get better here and as much as I miss you and wish I was home with you, coming here was the best thing I could have done."

She paused for a moment but continued on, "When Ray told me I should come here, I don't know, I still wasn't ready to admit that I needed help, but when you walked in and asked me to do it, I finally realized just how far down I had gone. So, thank you both for helping me see that I needed this and for being so strong and supportive of me." By this time, there were tears rolling down her cheek.

Lance wrapped his arms around her and said, "Don't cry momma I want you to be happy."

"Oh, Lance, it's not that I'm not happy. I'm getting happier all the time." Hope said. "These tears aren't so much sad tears as they are tears of regret. I'm so sorry that it took me so long to see it. But I'm getting better every day and when I'm all better, I'm going to come home, and we'll get things back on track. I'm thinking I might look for a job that I can do while you're in school so I can be there at night just to keep from sitting around all the time thinking. At night, I want to be there to help you with your homework and sit down to dinner together."

"Will it be okay if I have a dog?" Lance asked.

"Tell me about this dog?" Hope asked. "I've heard you were trying to befriend one."

"He's a great dog, mom." Lance began. "I named him Lucky because I would be so lucky if he's my dog. He's not real big, but he's not one of those really little ones either. He's kind of scared of people, but he's not afraid of me anymore. He lets me pet him. He is great at fetch."

"I think maybe he was someone's pet at one point, but something happened that he doesn't have them anymore." Ray explained. "I don't know if they moved away or what." He didn't want to add that it was possible the person had died. "Anyway, whatever caused him to lose his people, I'm guessing he's been on his own for a while and maybe someone did something to make him less trusting. We do know that before we started feeding him, he used to rummage Sally's garbage scrounging for food. I'm sure Sally was never unkind, but that may not have been the case with everyone. Maybe some weren't as friendly about him hanging around. He'd become pretty timid, but Lance is winning him over." Ray really hoped that she would be okay with Lance claiming the dog, it had become the only thing Lance had to hang onto for a while.

"I'm sure we can work it out." Hope said. "We'll see how things are when I come home. If he's been on his own for a long time, he may not want to be confined in a house, but we'll at least make sure he gets fed and cared for."

Lance threw his arms around his mother and said, "Thanks mom! He'll be a great dog, you'll see."

Ray could tell that while Hope was very happy to see her son, she still had a lot on her mind and things to sort through before she would be completely back to herself. When Lance jumped or became excited, there was the slightest flinch, like maybe she was still having some problems with adjusting her nerves without the aid of the drugs. He could tell that she really wanted to engage, but there was still that part that had become so used to doing everything high that relearning how to interact completely sober was still a work in progress.

Hope offered to give them a tour of the facility and although Ray had one before, he eagerly accepted. There were two reasons for that, one was that he wanted to be able to give encouragement about things and the other was that he wanted to see the place through Hope and Lance's eyes.

She showed them the common areas like the TV room and the kitchen and dining room, she pointed down one hallway and said down there is where we have our meetings and things. She didn't go into much detail about that, most likely because she didn't want to have to tell Lance a lot of what happened there. She showed them her room upstairs and showed Lance the photo viewer that Ray had gotten her.

She put the flowers on the small nightstand right beside her bed. Ray had suggested that Lance get something that came in its own vase or pot so she wouldn't have to worry about keeping them in water.

Ray could tell that Hope had come to a point where she wasn't sure what else to talk about. Most likely she didn't want to share everything with her son and right now, her entire focus had to be on getting better and avoiding going back to her former ways. He decided to try to take both of their minds off of the awkwardness for a while. "Hey, I have my camera down in the car, why don't I go grab it and we can take some photos in the yard or whatever. I can send them to you, Hope and you can see them whenever you want, Lance. We can maybe even print some for you to have in your room for now."

"Yeah!" Lance yelled, "Let's take pictures mom. The first one needs to be you holding your flowers." They sat on her small loveseat and waited for Ray to get his camera.

On the way out to his vehicle, Kelly stopped him for a minute. "How's it going?"

"Pretty good. I'm going to get my camera to take some pictures of Hope and Lance. How's she doing from your perspective?"

"She's doing well. Obviously, she has a ways to go, but choosing to take the medications helped a lot with the withdraw symptoms. Now it's a matter of focusing on learning different ways to cope with her grief and how to deal with the things that her addiction may have caused like distancing herself and losing relationships."

"I'm happy to hear she's doing well."

"I was coming to see if you and Lance would be interested in having lunch with us." she asked.

"I, uh." Ray hesitated. He wasn't sure if Lance would be exposed to anything that might make him apprehensive or scared if someone was going through a difficult withdraw or something like that.

"If you're worried about Lance, everyone does detox in their room. No one comes to lunch in the dining room until they are past the withdraw. It's difficult for other residents to see that tool." Kelly assured. "It will be ready by one, so you can go enjoy your picture taking."

"Okay, I'm sure he'd love to eat with his mom." Ray said. He continued out to his car and grabbed his camera. When he went upstairs, Lance and his mom were talking about what all he had been doing to catch up on his schoolwork. "Kelly asked if we'd like to stay for lunch. I said yes, I hope that's okay with you." He looked from Lance to Hope trying to make sure that they both knew the last part was for both of them. He couldn't really read Hope's reaction. "She said we have about forty-five minutes to take some pictures before we have to go for lunch. So, why don't we do a few here with the flowers and then maybe head outside to find some nice backgrounds."

It seemed like the activity was making Hope a little more relaxed. It was hard not to have fun with Lance being excited and wanting this pose and that pose and 'oh, let's do one by that tree' or 'I want one with us making silly faces'. Hope was more than happy to oblige every request that Lance had.

When their time was almost up, Hope made a request. "Could we do one by the sign?" she asked softly.

At first, Ray wasn't sure he had heard her right. So he asked, "You want one by the sign?"

"I do." she said a little more firmly. "I want it to be a reminder of where I am and what I have to work for."

"Sure." Ray said. They headed to where the sign was and took a few different poses. Just as they were finishing up, a woman came to the door to let them know that lunch was ready.

Ray hadn't been sure what to expect at lunch, but it turned out to be fun. The women all wanted to know who he and Lance were. They asked questions about Ray's decision to travel. They asked Lance about his schoolwork. It was obvious to Ray that Hope had talked about her son to these ladies. They knew about Lucky although they didn't know his name, but they knew Lance was trying to win over a stray.

Ray knew that some were probably close to being finished with rehab and others were just nicely getting started, but it was obvious that they all were supportive of each other's journey. When they were finished eating, one of the women told Hope, "How about you and I trade, I'll take your lunch dishes and you take my laundry folding later? That way you can visit longer."

"Sure, thanks Cindy." Hope said with a smile.

They spent another hour or so in the TV room visiting with Hope and a couple of the other ladies before heading back home.

On the ride home, Ray said, "It seems like there's a lot of nice people there."

"Yeah." Lance agreed happily. "I'm glad my mom has friends to be with."

Lance talked a lot about his mom and all the photos they had taken. "Can we send my mom a picture of Lucky?" he asked. "Afterall, when she gets home, Lucky will be her dog too. I want her to see what a great dog he is."

"Sure, we can do that." Ray agreed, "We'll take one when we get back, we have to go and feed him anyway."

After they fed Lucky, Lance sat on the ground and was able to get the dog to sit next to him, sort of. They weren't touching, but the dog did sit and let his picture be taken. They went to a picnic table and sorted through the photos on Ray's camera. He didn't want to overwhelm Hope and fill up her device so quickly, so they only sent a few for now. Of course, the picture of Lucky was in there. For the most part, Ray let Lance chose the photos to send, but he picked the one where Hope looked the happiest and healthiest to him and sent that. He was hoping that the woman could see the changes in herself from the photos taken at the diner before she left, and the ones taken that day. Her weeks in rehab had already started making a difference.

# Chapter 14

It was a Monday, one week before school was set to start and they were feeding Lucky in the evening. It seemed like Lance had a lot on his mind. Ray wanted to know what was bothering him, so he started throwing some topics out there. His friends had all come back from camp a couple of weeks before, and they often joined in on the basketball or baseball games with Ray. He really liked the group of friends Lance had. He had no fear that once Hope was home, Lance would feel less sad about him having to move on, He had his own tribe of people and even now, there were times when the boys were hanging out and doing things and Ray wasn't involved. That was a good thing. Hope was doing well, Lance had been able to see her every weekend, sometimes Ray had taken him, sometimes Sally and Steve had taken him and one time they had all gone together. So, in Ray's mind, he should have been fairly happy about how life was going right now.

"You did really great on catching up on the schoolwork, Lance. You'll get to move on with your friends." Ray encouraged.

"Yeah, I know, I was talking to the guys the other day." the boy said. "They're all excited that I'll be in middle school with them next year."

"Your mom's doing great, it won't be a whole lot longer until she gets to come home." he said.

"Yeah, it will be great to have her home." Lance agreed. "I can't wait. I like it at Aunt Sally's, but I want to be home with my mom soon."

"You will be." Ray assured. He was wracking his brain trying to figure out what had Lance in a somber mood. But he wasn't going to grill the kid, if

Lance wanted him to know, he would tell him. He decided to just let it be for now and see if Lance gave him any clue. He did, but not directly. Ray overheard him talking to Lucky.

“I was really hoping you’d be my dog by now, Lucky.” he began. “I know you come and sit by me and stuff when I’m here, but I was hoping you’d be mine and come home with me. Not my house, but my Aunt Sally’s for now.” He took a long pause and rubbed behind the dog’s ear. “I start school next Monday, and I probably won’t be able to come here to see you and feed you in the mornings. I know Ray will, until he has to go away, but I’m worried that you won’t get taken care of as much. I wanted to start school being able to tell everybody I have a dog.”

Well, now Ray knew what was making Lance sad, he just didn’t know what to do about it. Until the dog was ready, there wasn’t much they could do to change its mind. He would be here for several more weeks and would take care of the dog in the mornings, but when he left, he wasn’t sure what the dog would do if it wasn’t comfortable with going to Lance’s house. Maude wouldn’t be able to make the trip to the park every day. Sally and Steve would be busy with opening the diner each morning. They generally had a fairly large breakfast crowd. Hope would be back before Ray left, but he wasn’t sure she would want to make an every morning trek to the park after getting Lance off to school and she had been talking more and more about getting a job to keep her busy when she got home. It really would be up to the dog if he wanted to have a family to take care of him or not.

They sat until it was starting to get dark, the streetlights would be coming on soon. “It’s time to head out.” Ray said.

“Yeah.” Lance said somberly. He got up and started to walk in the direction of his aunt’s house. When he did though, the most amazing thing happened. He didn’t even see it because he was kind of sulking and had his face turned down.

Ray saw it though, and he couldn’t believe it. “Lance, turn around.” he said.

The boy turned and realized that Lucky was following about three steps behind him. “You coming home, boy?” he asked. “Come on, let’s go home.” He waved his hand to encourage the dog to follow and it did. Somehow, either it understood what Lance had been saying to it, or it had just decided that it was ready to have a family and a home to go to. Either way, it was making a boy very happy.

They walked to Sally and Steve's house, Lucky trailed them the whole way. When they arrived, the dog seemed apprehensive about going into the house, but he lay down in the front yard. Ray wasn't sure what the homeowners felt about having a dog in their house anyway, so the front yard or front porch were probably best for now anyway.

"You sit here on the porch, Lance, I'll be right back." Ray said, heading back in the direction of the park. He had left his SUV there because he wanted to walk with Lance since the dog was following him. He had been pretty sure that the dog wouldn't have gotten into the vehicle. He drove his vehicle the few blocks it took to get to Lance. He got in the back and took out the dog dish and the dog food. He told Lance, "We'll leave this here now, so you can feed him when you are supposed to. That way he gets used to being fed here."

"I know we fed him tonight already, but could we maybe give him a treat or some more food for being such a good dog and following me home?" Lance asked.

"Sure, we can do that." Ray agreed. "That's a really good idea." He sat the bowl and food on the porch and got out the bag of treats. "See if he'll come to you for it first, if not you can move closer to him. But I want to see if he'll come up here on the porch. If he feels comfortable on the porch, it will at least give him a place to eat and some shade during the day." Ray moved a few feet further down the porch so he wouldn't be the reason the dog didn't come to the porch.

Lance took one of the treats from the bag and held it out a little for Lucky to see. The dog began wagging his tail, he recognized what the boy had. "Come on, boy. Come and get the treat." The dog didn't jump and run, but it did slowly and timidly reach the porch. He took the treat out of Lances hand and lay on the ground at his feet to eat it. Lance laid another treat on the porch next to him. The dog would have to jump on the porch to be able to get to it. It was hesitant for a little while, and paced a little, never taking his eyes off of the treat.

Finally, it got the confidence to jump up on the porch and grab the treat. It had just gotten the jerky in its mouth when Steve and Sally pulled up from their day at the diner. Ray was worried about what the dog would do, he feared it might bolt at the newcomers, he had only met them once to Ray's knowledge. Instead of bolting away like Ray had thought it might, it just huddled itself close to Lance.

"Well, what do we have here?" Steve asked.

"I hope it's okay, Lucky just followed me home." the boy said timidly.

"It's perfectly fine." Sally said with a smile, "We've been wondering when he would give up his fear enough to come over."

"So, he can stay?" Lance asked excitedly.

"He can stay." Steve said, "For now, we'll feed him out here and let him know he's welcome. Maybe on Sunday we can see if he wants to come into the house. We don't know if he's housebroke so we want to be around the first time to make sure we keep an eye out for him going to the bathroom."

"Okay" Lance agreed. "That's great, did you hear that Lucky, this is your house for now. You can stay here on the porch and I'll feed you every morning before school and every night at dinnertime." The dog perked up its ears and nudged Lance on his arm. It wasn't ready to greet the others yet, but it wasn't so fearful that it ran and hid either.

"Well, I should get back to Maude's" Ray said. "The dishes are there beside the food. I bought two, but we never wanted to leave anything in the park so we really only used one for both food and water."

"Thanks for bringing everything over and for helping Lance get himself a dog." Sally said.

"No thanks necessary." Ray said. He walked to his SUV and turned to wave at his friends before he got in and drove to his temporary home for now. It was only a few blocks, but he took a longer route so that he could drive past Hope's house. He had gotten the lawn mowed and had hired a teenager to keep up on doing it at least until Hope got back. When she was home, she could decide if she kept on paying the kid or not. He parked and got out, he took a walk around the building to make sure none of the windows looked like they had been tampered with. Barbara had peeked out her front window and given him a brief wave. As much as he generally didn't love a busybody, he had to admit that her form of neighborhood watch seemed to be effective. He walked around the house and didn't see anything amiss, so he got into his vehicle and drove to Maude's. He sat with her watching television for a while.

"How was your day?" Maude asked.

"It was a pretty good day." Ray said. "Lance's dog followed him home tonight. I guess it finally decided that he wanted to belong to someone."

"Oh, that's wonderful." Maude said. "He talks about that dog all the time. I know he has family and friends, but sometimes a dog can be the best thing for a kid."

"Definitely" Ray agreed. "When I first met Lance, there were times I'd see him talking to that dog and I would have given anything to know what he was saying. I didn't know his situation, but I was pretty sure it wasn't a great one. That dog knew it all though. Even though he couldn't let himself fully trust anyone, he'd sit and listen to Lance for as long as the boy would talk."

"They bonded." Maude said.

"I'm pretty sure that dog understands a lot more than we think he does." Ray began. "Today Lance was telling him how he was starting school soon and how he wished the dog would come up with him. When Lance got up and started walking, the dog just followed him."

"I think animals do understand us." Maude said. "Oh, not the actual words maybe, but they understand the heart."

"I'm pretty sure you're right, Maude."

Maude said, "I think I'm headed to bed. I'll see you in the morning, Ray."

"Goodnight, Maude."

Before he fell asleep, he spent some time thinking about what his future looked like. Being here and seeing this close knit community had made him think a lot about family and the fact that as Maude had pointed out several times, family didn't have to be blood. There were people in this town that he already considered family in a way, but he did have blood out there. He a cousin he hadn't seen in years. They used to be close when they were kids. But when Ray's dad had left, he didn't see that side of the family anymore. He had a half-brother he had never met. Should he meet him, did he want that connection. He had thought years ago that he never wanted to meet the man because his existence had come out of so much hurt for Ray's mom. But he had to admit to himself, that the guy hadn't had a hand in that hurt. He had been a product of their father making choices that hurt both Ray and his mom. But he had been innocent in it all. It was something he would think about until he got a real sense of what was best, he wasn't going to make a quick decision.

He wasn't going to fall asleep easily with so much on his mind, so he decided to pull out his table and see if he could find out anything about either man. It took a while of going down rabbit holes on social media, but he eventually found both men. He jotted down what city they lived in and figured he would have time to think about whether or not he wanted to find either one of them.

# Chapter 15

The following morning, Ray took a route that would take him past the park, but he hoped Lucky wasn't there which would also likely mean that Lance wouldn't be there. He was really hoping that the dog had fully chosen for Lance to be his boy. No one was at the park, that was a good sign. He drove over to Steve's house and sure enough, Lance and Lucky were sitting on the porch together. The dog alerted when Ray got out of the car, but he didn't seem overly worried once he saw who was there. Ray still wasn't planning to leave until Hope got home, but he was feeling better all the time about how things were going for Lance.

"So, now that Lucky isn't hanging out in the park, what do you want to do today?" Ray asked as he sat next to Lance on the porch.

"I don't know, we could just play catch in the backyard, maybe." Lance said.

"That sounds like a good idea." Ray said.

They walked around the house to use the gate to get to the backyard instead of going through the house so that Lucky could follow if he wanted to. He followed right behind Lance as if it were what he had always done.

While they were playing catch, Lucky explored his new surroundings. He found a spot under a shade tree and laid down to watch them. After a few minutes, Lance asked, "Do you think my mom will be home by the fifteenth?"

"No, Lance," Ray said. "I don't think so. Why, what's the fifteenth?"

"My birthday." Lance said as if it were no big deal.

"I'm sure she'll be bummed that she can't be here." Ray said. "We can make a trip up there. I'll call and see if that day will be okay."

"Yeah." Lance agreed.

"Maybe we can have a party with some of your friends, too." Ray offered. "We'll talk to Sally about it when we go for lunch."

"Okay."

They played catch and Lance and Lucky played a little fetch before it was time to go get lunch. They walked out through the gate, and Lucky followed them. "No, you stay here, boy." Lance said. "I'll be back." But the dog still kept following him.

"It's okay Lance, Lucky knows his way around town, If he doesn't wait for us by the diner, I'm sure he'll either head back to the park or to the house." Ray assured. "We'll find him after lunch."

"Okay." Lance agreed. "I hope he doesn't get lost."

They walked to the diner, and the dog remained right behind them the whole way. When they walked in, he laid on the sidewalk out of the way of foot traffic and seemed like he was going to wait. Ray wasn't sure that he would stay the whole time, but if he didn't he should be easy to find later. Depending on whether or not one night had convinced him that he had a new home. Although, that was where his food and water were now, so he might associate it with that.

They ordered their lunch and Ray asked Sally if she had a minute. "Sure, let me go put in your order and I'll be right back."

When she came to the table, Ray began, "So, Lance tells me he has a birthday coming up. I am going to see if we can go see Hope, but I was wondering what you would think of a party for his friends?"

"I think that's a great idea!" Sally said. "Maybe we could get some pizza's from G's and have everyone over or we could have it here on a Sunday."

Ray was hoping that they could get him excited about some kind of a party. "How does that sound, Lance? I'd be willing to go pick up the pizza and breadsticks and stuff."

"Yeah, that sounds fun." Lance said. "I'd still like to see my mom though."

Ray said, "Let me step over there and call Kelly and see what they think." He got out of the booth and walked to a corner near the storage closet and dialed the number. "Hey, Kelly, it's Ray Hawthorne." he said when the woman answered.

"Hi Ray, what can I do for you?" she asked.

"Well, I'm not sure, but I figured I'd try." he began. "Lance has a birthday coming up and he'd really like to be able to spend it with his mom." He wanted to give the woman every reason to say yes and no reason to say no, so he continued, "I'd be glad to spring for the cake or whatever else we can do for a party."

"When is it?" she asked.

"The fifteenth."

"I'll talk to Hope to make sure that's going to be okay for her, but as long as she's up for it, we'll take care of it here. We have ladies that love to bake." Kelly said. "Would it be the four of you?"

"I'm not sure, I don't have a calendar in front of me, what day is the fifteenth?"

"It's a Sunday." she said.

"Well, then yeah, I'm thinking it will be the four of us." Ray said. "The diner is closed on Sunday, but I can let you know if it's not going to be all of us."

"It's fine either way. I was just curious." Kelly said. "I wanted to see how Hope feels."

"If she's uncomfortable with any of it, we'll change the plan." Ray said. "Lance will understand if it's not going to be okay for her. He may be disappointed, but he'll understand. He knows his mom's recovery is top priority right now."

"Great, I'll let you know in the next day or two." Kelly said and then she ended the call.

When Ray walked back to the table, he didn't want to let on that the party may not happen because of Hope, so he just said, "Kelly's going to look at the calendar and stuff and get back to me."

"I hope it works out." Lance said.

"I know you do, Lance, but your mom's recovery is top priority right now, right?" Ray asked.

"Yeah. It is." Lance agreed.

"Well, if we can't have a party with her right now, we'll have a coming home and birthday party combined when she gets home. Okay?" Sally asked.

"Okay." Lance agreed. "I think we should have a coming home party either way. Mom's working really hard to get better and she deserves a party."

"I agree, but, that's also got to be up to your mom." Sally said. "She may not be ready to have a bunch of people around and we don't want to overwhelm her right away."

"I guess." Lance said he didn't sound like he fully agreed with their assessment.

"Either way, we'll do something special for her." Ray said. "If she's not up to a bunch of people, we'll have a special dinner just for us or something like that."

Lance just nodded his agreement.

After they finished their lunch, they walked back out and Ray was happy to see that Lucky was indeed waiting for them in the exact spot he had taken up before they entered the diner. When he saw Lance, he stood up and wagged his tail. "Good boy, Lucky." Lance exclaimed and gave the dog a good ear rub and a hug. “Wanna go to the park and see if any of my friends are there?”

Ray wasn’t sure if Lance was talking to him or to the dog, but he said, “Sure that sounds like a plan.” And they headed down the road. When they got to the corner where Lance’s temporary home would have been to the right and the park was to the left, the dog seemed a little confused when they didn’t head toward home, but he followed his boy anyway.

At the park, there was indeed a group of boys playing catch. Lance went to join in so Ray and Lucky found a spot at a picnic table. The dog got up after a bit and walked over to the water faucet. He looked to Lance, but when the boy didn’t notice him, he looked at Ray. Ray walked over and turned on the faucet and Lucky lapped away.

“You need to take good care of Lance when I’m gone.” Ray told the dog. “I know you know he’ll take care of you, but you need to be a good dog for him. You listen to all his secrets, you get excited when he’s happy and you mourn with him when he’s sad. He needs a good friend like you.”

The dog looked up at Ray and wagged his tail. Ray wasn’t sure if that was a thanks for turning on the water or if it was the dog’s agreement to what he had said. Either way, he did believe that the dog was one hundred percent Lance’s dog now and would be as loyal to him as any dog had ever been.

The boys all agreed to meet the following day at the school since Ray had a basketball they could play with. They met either at the school or the park every day except Sunday as some of them went to church and some of them didn’t, but it was also the last day before school was to start and many parents wanted the kids home for one last family day. The same was true for Lance, Steve and Sally took the opportunity to have a nice family day with a cook out and playing fetch and catch in their own yard.

Ray had decided to spend that Sunday with Maude. He wanted Lance to feel like his aunt and uncle truly were his family. Ray wanted the boy to feel like he had a strong bond with them so that when Ray moved on, he still believed he had a strong support system.

When Ray had told Maude he wanted to spend the day with her, she had offered to not go to church, but Ray had negated that idea and told her he would rather go with her than have her miss it. Maude always dressed up a little for church, so Ray had put on a suit. He wasn't sure if he would fit in with how others were dressed or not, but he remembered when he used to go to church as a youth, he had always been taught that you were supposed to give God your best and so he wore a suit.

Ray's family had never been overly religious, and more especially after his father left, church became something that his mom no longer put any effort into. Ray wasn't sure if it was because his mom felt like God hadn't cared about her if He allowed her husband to leave or if it was the embarrassment of having to go to church without him and explain why he wasn't there with them. Whatever her reasons, she didn't really attend anymore except on Christmas and Easter.

The people at the church were very welcoming, most of them had met Ray at one point or another in the weeks he had been here. They all said they were glad to see him. Ray wasn't sure if it would be called divine intervention or just a coincidence, but the minister spoke about relationships and loving one another. He spoke about forgiveness and not holding a grudge. It gave Ray a lot to think about in his debate of whether or not he wanted to meet his half-brother, and whether or not he should look up the cousin that had left his life when his father had left them.

After the service was over, Ray offered to take Maude anywhere she wanted for lunch. She thought for a moment and then said "Well, there's this nice place about twenty miles out of town that my husband always took me on special occasions or just when we needed a night out. I haven't been there in years. If it's still there, I'd love to go."

"What's the name of it?" Ray asked taking out his phone.

"Normandie's" Maude said.

Ray searched the name in his browser and found out that they were indeed open so he set up his GPS to take them there.

Over dinner, Ray told Maude, "I'm sure you know that I'll be leaving shortly after Hope gets home. I want to make sure that she gets settled before I move on, but I've already been here a lot longer than I ever planned to."

"Oh, I know you will, and we'll all miss you, but you've done so much for so many that I know you'll always have a place in so many hearts and you'll always have a room at my place if you want to come back for a visit, free of charge."

"No, I'll pay if I do come back, I don't want to burden anyone." Ray argued.

"You've given me more than any money would ever be worth, making it so that I can see my babies and grandbabies. But I won't argue with you about it now. Let's just enjoy our nice dinner." Maude said.

# Chapter 16

The fourteenth of the month, Steve and Sally had decided to leave the diner up to their staff after the lunch rush and they opened their backyard to all of Lance's friends for a huge birthday party. Lance was turning twelve, his last year as a preteen. They had Ray bring a bunch of pizzas and they had gotten a cake and ice cream along with beverages and munchies.

They were set up for yard games including a water balloon toss which quickly turned into a water balloon fight. They had other carnival type games too and each boy went home with a bag of goodies that Lance gave them as he said goodbye and thanked them for coming.

On Sunday, the four made the trip to see Lance's mom. Ray could tell that Lance was either excited or nervous about being with his mom. He was pretty sure it was excitement, but he had never really thought that Lance was super comfortable with being at the facility. Most young boys wouldn't feel like it was a fun place to hang out. Regardless of how much he wanted to be with his mom, it was pretty much just a place where they sat and talked, and Hope wasn't always sure what to say so conversations sometimes became stilted.

This day was apparently going to be different though. As soon as they pulled up to the door, Hope came out with two of the other residents behind her holding up a sign that said "Happy Birthday Lance!!" She looked very happy to see her son. Lance got out of the car and ran to his mom, she wrapped him in a long hug and kissed the top of his head. "Happy Birthday, Lance." she said. "I'm so happy it worked out for us to spend the day together."

"I am too, mom." Lance said with a huge smile.

They were all invited inside for lunch and someone had made a birthday cake too. "I asked them to make spaghetti." Hope said. "I know it's always been one of your favorites."

"It is!" Lance said.

They all ate while Lance answered questions from the ladies about his party the day before and how school was going. They all engaged with Lance as if they all had a vested interest in his life.

After they were done with the main course and Lance had blown out the candles on his cake, Hope said, "I got you a small present. I wasn't sure what you wanted, but I hope you like it." She handed him a small box wrapped in happy birthday paper.

Lance opened the box as if this would be the most important present he had received. He had gotten several from his friends the day before, but the adults had saved their gifts to give to him at his party with his mom. Ray hadn't been sure if Hope would have the ability to get a gift or not in her situation, but apparently, she had. When he pulled out a leather collar with a dog tag attached, he read the tag. It had Lucky's name on it along with his home address. "This is so cool mom!" Lance exclaimed. "We have a dog and now people will know where he belongs."

"We do have a dog." Hope agreed. "I don't know if you want to use it now, because it's not the address you are at, but it's definitely good for when I get home."

"Do you know when you're coming home mom?" Lance asked.

Hope glanced at Kelly before saying anything. "It should only be a couple more weeks, if everything keeps going good." Kelly had given her a slight nod and a big smile to encourage her to let her son know that there was a plan, but if it didn't work out, that would be okay too. It may take a little more time, but that wasn't likely. Hope was doing really well. Her son had been her motivation and that had been a strong reason for her to succeed.

"Would it be okay if we have a party for you when you come home?" Lance asked. "I'm sure everyone is dying to see you."

Hope looked like she was pondering that for a while. Ray wasn't sure if it was her fear of what people might think or say or if she just didn't want to be in a crowd of people for fear her nerves weren't ready for that yet.

"I'll tell you what," Sally said, having the same conundrum that Ray was having. "The Sunday you get home, we'll have a welcome home party at the diner. But you can let me know if you want it to be by invitation only or if you want it open to everyone. You think about it and let me know what you decide."

Hope smiled at the thoughtfulness of her sister-in-law and said, "Thank you, that sounds perfect. I'll think about it and give you a decision before the time comes."

Lance began to open the rest of his gifts, some of the other ladies had gotten him a card and placed small amounts of money in them. Sally and Steve had gotten him a DVD of a movie he loved and Ray had gotten him a small simple cellphone. He had checked with both Hope and Sally if it would be okay. When Lance opened it, Ray told him "I checked with your mom and your aunt and uncle before I got that. It's got my number already programmed into it so you can call me anytime after I leave. I'm not sure what the school's policy is on them, so you'll have to abide by that. But I wanted you to be able to reach me if you ever just want to talk."

"Thanks Ray!" Lance said excitedly. "I wish you didn't have to go away, but this will at least make it so I can talk to you."

Ray gave him a small smile, a wink and a nod of thanks and agreement. Ray had figured they would have lunch and open presents and the rest of the visit would consist of them sitting and chatting either outside or in the common areas. He was wrong. When the dishes were cleared, one of the other residents said "We have a few games out in the backyard if anyone wants to play. It's nothing super fancy, just a few things some of us thought of."

Lance and Hope eagerly agreed to the games. When they stepped outside, Ray was surprised to see that there were indeed several stations set up for different games, a bean bag toss, a couple of different relay type games, and each game had some small prize that was given to Lance whether he won or not since it was his birthday. Ray hung back and let the others play. He wanted to talk to Kelly, and he wanted them to come to enjoy being together as a family without him involved. The more they relied on each other and less on him, the easier it would be when he left.

“You guys really went all out for the party.” he said to Kelly.

“It was all the ladies’ idea.” Kelly began. “Some of them have kids, some of them don’t. Of the ones that have kids, most have lost them on some level because of their addictions. Some have literally lost them to the court system. Some have been given temporary guardians similar to what you got set up for Lance. They realize just what it means to have to miss your child’s birthday and if they could help Hope not to have to miss Lance’s, they were all for it. Some of the games might be a little childish for Lance, but they came up with them and I don’t think Lance will mind that they’re not all targeted to his age group, I think it’s about spending time having fun with his mom.” She gave a nod across the yard to suggest Ray turn and see what she meant.

Ray turned to see Lance and his mom doing a three legged race with their feet tied together. They weren’t making much progress because they were both laughing and trying to remain upright, which they didn’t always do, and that just caused more laughter.

Everyone was having so much fun going from station to station and back to their favorites, that no one was paying attention to the time. Finally, someone said “Oh, crap, we need to get started on dinner.”

Ray looked at Kelly and said, “I don’t want to cross any boundaries here, but under the circumstances, I’d be glad to have pizza delivered on my dime so that everyone can continue to enjoy their day.” Kelly agreed and she and Ray went inside to order the pizza. When it arrived, everyone sat around the tables and chairs in the yard and laughed and joked and had a good time. When they were done, everyone thanked Ray. Some decided to go to their rooms, some decided to go watch Lance’s new movie and some decided to stay in the yard a little while longer. Ray had a feeling that the ones that wanted to go to their rooms might, at least in part, be the ones who had their own children that they weren’t able to see right now for one reason or another. But he couldn’t be sure of that, it was just a hunch.

On the ride home, Lance talked non-stop about how much fun he had. He was worried about Lucky though, but they had finally gotten him used to the back yard and the gate being closed so that he couldn’t always follow

Lance everywhere. They had left a small amount of food and plenty of water and he would get the rest of his food when they got home.

By the time Lance had fed Lucky and given him some attention, it was time for Lance to get ready for bed. He had school tomorrow. Ray said goodnight and headed back to Maude's house.

Almost five weeks after Lance's birthday, Ray received a phone call from Kelly. Hope was ready to come home, but she had requested that Ray come alone to pick her up. He wasn't sure why she had asked that, but Kelly said that it was in part due to the fact that Hope wanted to surprise her son and she had some things that she wanted to take care of before she saw him. Ray was more than happy to go along with whatever worked best for Hope.

He helped her load her things into his SUV, she signed the paperwork that finalized her treatment, got the schedule for support meetings in her area and they were on their way back to Thousand Palms.

"I want to go to my house and make sure everything is gone, and I wanted you there with me when I do it, if that's okay." Hope began after several minutes in the car. "I know Sally and the ladies gave it a thorough cleaning, but I want to check all of my old hidey-holes and be sure. If I find anything, I want you to take it and get rid of it."

"I'd be glad to help with that." Ray agreed. Now he knew why Hope had been adamant that she didn't want anyone but Ray to come to pick her up. She hadn't wanted to take a chance on her son seeing what she found, if she found anything.

When they arrived at her house, she immediately went in search of anything that may have been left behind. Fortunately, she didn't find anything. "What did you do with everything that was found?" she asked. "I hope it was disposed of properly."

"I thought about just trying to dispose of it, but I don't really know much about what could happen if it were in a drain system and I definitely didn't want to just throw it in a dumpster. So, I took it to the local sheriff and told him I had found it somewhere. He didn't ask too many questions." Ray said.

"Oh, I'm pretty sure he knew where you found it." Hope said. "I don't think many people around here didn't have at least some clue as to what I was doing. I'm fortunate that I never did anything to give them a reason to come and search. But I've learned my lesson. There we so many times that I tried to stop. I knew I needed to stop for Lance, but I just couldn't do it on my own. It really takes over your life and in ways you never even expected or thought could happen to you."

"I've known a few people over the years with an addiction and I've seen some make it and I've seen some not make it. I'm very happy that you are one of the ones that did." Ray said. "Lance is a good kid, and he deserves to have a happy home. If you ever get overwhelmed, you have people here who want to help. You can call me, but I know that Steve and Sally and even Maude would be glad to do what they can."

"I know, and I should have reached out to someone a long time ago. I know that Steve was hurting from the loss of his brother, but instead of seeing him as someone that I could lean on, I thought I was protecting him from more hurt by not adding to his burden." Hope said. "I know now that was the wrong way to handle things. I just went down a deep dark hole and eventually I couldn't see my way out and I couldn't ask anyone to help me find it either. It starts out as something you do once or twice just to give you a break from the pain. But then the fact that the pain comes back makes you want more so you can keep the pain at bay for just a little while longer. After a while though, the spiral keeps going. When I first started, I'd smoke a joint once in a while, just to get a little bit of time away from what was going on in my own head. Then I was smoking them more often and eventually, it wasn't enough. I needed something stronger, and the dealer was more than happy to upgrade me. He knew exactly what he was doing too. He offered me my first taste for free, just so I could see if I liked it. And oh did I like it. It gave me that peace again, or at least I thought it did. But it always wears off and then you need more. It was like I could see exactly what I was doing to myself and to my son, but I didn't know how to stop it without the pain overtaking me. One of the things they told me I need to do is try to explain to people that I care about is what happened and how I started down that spiral. I know I need to tell Lance, at least on some level so he understands. I hope that what I tell him will not only let him see that I wasn't doing it because I wanted to, at some point, it became something I needed no matter what that meant to anyone else. I realize that I'm very fortunate that I didn't lose Lance, some of the women at the center did. The courts took them away at least temporarily and ordered them into rehab. While I was there, two different women decided it wasn't worth it and they walked away from the program. As soon as the drugs started to flush out of my system, I knew there was no way I wasn't going to stay and finish, for myself and for Lance. He means too much to me to not have stayed. I know it didn't seem that way when you first came to town, but it was always in there somewhere, I just had to find it again."

"Well, I'm glad you had the chance to see what was important and you took the steps needed to get it back." Ray said.

"I don't think I would have if you hadn't shown up though." Hope said.

"I'm happy for whatever part I played in it. But you're the one who did the work once you took the path toward recovery." Ray said. "Hey it's almost time for Lance to get out of school, do you want to go pick him up?"

Hope thought about that for a minute and decided "No, I'd rather stay here and have you go get him and bring him home. I know his stuff is still at Steve's, and we'll have to work out how the transition is going to go, but I want to surprise him by being here."

"Okay. I'll go pick him up then." Ray said. When he got in his car, he gave Sally a quick call. He knew she wouldn't have a problem with Lance going home to see his mother, but he wanted her to at least be aware of the change in plans. He had told her when he got the call about Hope being released. Sally said that she and Steve would leave early and let the staff take care of closing the diner. They wanted to have a small family diner including Ray to celebrate Hope's first night home.

Lance was surprised to see Ray waiting for him by the school's doors. He walked over to his friend and said "What are you doing here? Is everything okay?"

"Yeah, things are fine." Ray said. "I just wanted to give you a ride home."

"Oh, okay." Lance sounded relieved that there wasn't a problem.

When Ray turned the wrong way for taking Lance to Steve and Sally's house, he was puzzled. Ray said, "I just wanted to do a drive-by to make sure everything looks good at your house. I do it most days."

"I didn't know that.." Lance said. When they got close enough that he could see the front porch, Lance saw his mom sitting on the step. He shouted with excitement, "She's home! My mom's home!"

"She is, I picked her up just a little while ago." Before Ray had the car shut off, Lance was jumping out and running to hug his mom.

"You're home!" Lance said wrapping his arms around his mother's waist and burying his face in her shoulder. Hope wasn't a tall woman and Lance was already as tall as she was.

"I'm home." Hope said, cradling her son to her. "And I'm never going back."

Ray told them both about the invitation for all of them to go to Sally's house for a welcome home dinner, so they decided to go over there now so Hope could get to know Lucky. As soon as they got there, Lance took Hope out to the backyard and said, "See boy, I told you she would be back soon. My mom's home so now we can all go back to our house." Over the time that Lucky had been living here, he had pretty much become a normal loving dog. He had realized that the people who surrounded him now, weren't going to hurt him and he was settled. He had proven that he either had been house trained before or he just caught on really quickly because it had taken no time at all for him to be trusted in the house. If the weather was nice, they still left him in the yard when no one was home though so they didn't have to worry about accidents and he had room to run.

Ray was never sure if the dog was understanding everything Lance was saying or if he just had a really good memory because he greeted Hope as if he trusted her fully because his boy loved her and that was all the recommendation he needed.

"Hey, Lucky." Hope said putting out her hand for the dog to sniff. He sniffed her hand for a brief second before he decided that she was okay, so he rubbed his head against her hand for some good ear rubs. Since he had come home with Lance, he had become a very well behaved and loving dog. "He's got the collar I bought him on."

"Yeah, the address is wrong, but I think everyone in town knows that I have been staying here for now." Lance said.

Ray didn't think that Lance had noticed, but he hadn't missed the look on Hope's face at that statement. She was likely regretting the fact that everyone in town probably knew exactly what had happened to her and she was afraid they would be judging her. He really hoped that they wouldn't be harsh, but one never knew what people would do. Either way, he wasn't leaving for a week or two to be sure that everything seemed to settle in and return to the way it should have always been.

# Chapter 17

Sally brought home a large pot of white chicken chili and a bag of tortilla chips. They sat around the table to eat, and she said, "I hope you like this; Lance seems to really enjoy it."

"It's great mom, wait till you try it." Lance said.

Hope smiled and said, "I've heard rave reviews, so it must be amazing."

While they ate, they talked about how school was going for Lance. How well things were going now that they had extra help at the diner, and the goings on around their small town.

When they were done, Hope offered to help Sally clear the table. When they were in the kitchen she said "I just wanted to thank you for everything. There are so many things I can't begin to name them all. I really appreciate you getting ladies together to clean my house before I came home."

Sally gave her a brief hug and said, "Oh, it's not been a problem at all. Just so you know, I cleaned your bedroom all by myself. I figured it was only right that family took care of your personal stuff."

Hope knew exactly what that meant. Sally had been the only one to find her stash of drugs. She had assumed that they would be in the bedroom because Hope wanted to keep them from being found by Lance, so she had stored them among her private things. "Thank you for that. I know everyone in town kind of knows, but I appreciate you being the one to clean it all up."

"I gave the bag to Ray, and I am not sure what happened to it from there, but I knew it didn't need to be there when you came home." Sally said. "I'm so sorry that we didn't reach out to you sooner. I think we just didn't know how. Steve was so devastated by the loss of his brother that he went into his own dark place for a while. I was so busy trying to help him that I didn't see what was happening with you until I felt like it was too late. I know now that it wouldn't have been too late, and I should have stepped up anyway. I'm so sorry that I didn't, but I am so thankful that Ray did."

"I don't know that I would have let you help me anyway." Hope began. "When those men showed up at my door, the minute I saw them in their dress uniforms, I just knew. I went numb, when the numbness started to wear off, I wanted to stay numb or high or whatever made me not have to think about what those men told me that day. I couldn't handle it. I missed him so much that I just couldn't see what I was doing to myself and to my son."

"Well, you aren't the first person to go down that path and I'm sure you won't be the last." Sally said. "But promise me that you'll come to us if you start feeling that way again. I know Steve was a mess too and you thought you would just make it harder on him, but we're family and you should be able to come to us. I know Steve regrets that he wasn't there for you and for Lance. But we're back on track and we will work together to stay there."

"Thank you." Hope said. "I think getting a part time job might help. That way I'm not home just sitting there all the time thinking. Maybe something I can do while Lance is in school. I want to be home to help him with schoolwork if he needs it, but sitting in that house all day alone just gives me time to think and that's not always a good thing."

"Well, we'd be happy to have you at the diner, but if that's too much family time, I totally understand." Sally said. "We'd work out a schedule that fits with whatever you need."

"That's very generous of you." she said.

"You know, I realized that we really don't know much about your family." Sally said. "We should have asked; we should have gotten to know you better."

"Well, there's not a lot to tell." Hope said. "I never talked about them because we weren't close really. My parents died just before I went off to college. I have a sister, but we weren't close growing up, she was a lot older than me. She still lives in Michigan with her family. She married a wealthy man and has never really had much time for me. When I met Paul, I was a silly college girl, and he was this handsome Marine. He was so kind and so charismatic. He was bigger than life and I was instantly attracted to him. We didn't have a long courtship, but I fell hard and fast."

"All we knew was we had never heard of you and then Paul was bringing you home as his new bride." Sally said. "I admit, we were a little baffled. Steve was worried you were just latching on to his brother because he was a Marine, some women do that. But once we met you, we knew that you truly loved Paul. I think Steve was just so protective of his brother."

"Paul told me that Steve practically raised him in a lot of ways." Hope said.

"He did, and that's why his brother's death was so hard on him." Sally said. "But that's no excuse for the fact that we didn't take the time to get closer to you. I guess with the fact that Paul was always away, we kind of let you slip through the cracks most of the time. I always enjoyed the times we all got together. I should have taken more time to build a bond that had nothing to do with whether or not Paul was here. I definitely plan to try to do better." Sally said.

"Well, I did my part in keeping a distance, especially after Paul died." Hope said. "I isolated myself and I know that I can't do that. I have to be more open to letting people in. I can't let hurt from the past make me close myself off now."

"We'll both make a better effort in the future." Sally said. "Did you ever finish college?"

"No, and that's something else I want to look into." Hope said. "I can't go back to campus, because of Lance, but I am going to see what's available online."

"That's great." Sally said. "Anything we can do to help, you just let us know."

"I appreciate that."

Lance was still set on having a coming home party with the whole town, but Hope told him that she didn't want to make a big deal of it all. She just wanted to settle into life and maybe find a part time job to keep herself busy and take a class or two online. Lance packed up his things and put them in Ray's SUV to be taken back home, but he insisted that he walk Lucky there, so he was sure to know where to go. Hope walked with them. They unpacked Lance's things and showed Lucky where his food and water would be available from now on.

Ray invited them to go to breakfast at Sally's the next morning and then they could go grocery shopping since pretty much everything had been thrown out so it didn't expire.

When he got back to Maude's, he told her that he wouldn't be there for breakfast the next morning, but she was welcome to join them at Sally's. She told him she might stop by but not to wait on her, they should go ahead and enjoy their breakfast.

When they got to the diner, Sally seated them at a table kind of in the middle of the diner. Ray wasn't sure why she had done that, because she usually allowed her customers to choose their own spot unless it was more crowded. But they sat at the table she suggested. It didn't take Ray long to figure out why though. They had barely gotten their order placed when Hope's neighbor Mrs. Johnson came into the diner and made her way to their table.

"Hope, I heard you were back." she said brightly. Ray thought it was more likely that she had seen Hope home, because she tended to be a nosy neighbor, but he didn't say anything and she continued. "I'm so glad you're home. Listen, I know you probably haven't had a chance to grocery shop, so I whipped up a couple of small casseroles that you can just heat and eat or they stay good in the freezer for quite a while too." She handed over two medium sized baking dishes.

"Thank you so much, Mrs. Johnson." Hope said. "I really appreciate that; I haven't had a chance to get to the store yet."

"Oh, you call me Barbara," the woman countered. "We're neighbors after all. If there's ever anything I can do, you just let me know." She walked away and set at one of the booths.

It was just a few minutes later when Mrs. Lawson, one of Lance's former teachers came in and stopped by their table. "Hope, it's so good to see you again." she began. "I know you probably haven't had enough time to do any real grocery shopping so I made a couple of pots of stew that you can heat up or put in the freezer for later." She sat two large storage bowls with lids on the table.

"Thank you so much, Mrs. Lawson." Hope said. "I really appreciate it."

"Oh, it's fine, dear." the woman said. "I know how it is to have an empty refrigerator to fill."

She walked over and sat at a booth with Mrs. Johnson, and they began talking over cups of coffee.

Another woman walked in and came to their table, Ray couldn't remember her name, he had only met her once. "Oh, Hope, I heard you were here. It's so good to have you home." she said. "I was doing a bunch of baking and I figured you could use some fresh bread and cookies. So, I made up a few extra."

One by one, women came in and offered up some sort of casserole or baked good until the diner was full of people sharing a cup of coffee and small talk. Hope was overwhelmed. Sally had taken the dishes and stored them in the big refrigerator in the back because Hope wouldn't have room for it all at once.

"Why are they all being so good to me?" she asked. "How did they even know I was home?"

"Oh, I think the answer to the second part just walked in the door." Sally said with a wink.

Hope turned to see Maude making her way to their table. "Welcome home Hope." she said. "Ray said you were home. I wanted to bring you a few things to help you get settled in. You can put them in the freezer to have whenever you want them."

"Why did you do all of this?" Hope asked with tears running down her face.

Maude rounded the table and pulled the young woman in for a hug. "Oh, sweet girl. I just made a few phone calls, not a person in this town didn't jump at the chance to come and welcome you back. Not a one of them was asked to make a single thing for you, they all offered. You're family to me Hope, not by blood, but that son of yours has spent time working at my table and I feel like he's just as special to me as any one of my own flesh and blood. You hit a rough patch, and made some choices that weren't the best, but no one in this room hasn't made mistakes in their past. Not a one of us is perfect and not a one of us wouldn't want others to reach out to us and offer help. I know it's hard to ask sometimes, but in this room, you see a bunch of people who are offering to be there if you ever need help again."

# Chapter 18

Hope had been home for a couple of weeks and things had settled in nicely in the small town. Lance had his dog, it slept by his bed every night and waited patiently for him on the porch at the end of the school day to go to the park and play fetch or even just sit and observe while Lance played with his friends. Lucky was always ready to retrieve a missed catch though.

Ray was going to be leaving the next morning, so Sally had declared the diner closed a couple of hours early to have a going away party for him. Although it was still open to who ever wanted to stop by and give him their well wishes or thanks for the things he had done.

Mrs. Cooper was the first to come and talk to him. She thanked him for all that he had done to help Lance pass on to the next grade. “I was hoping someone would step up and do it. I wanted to just pass the boy, but the school wouldn’t let me do that without a certain percentage of the missed work being done.” she said. “I know he’s a smart boy, but his world fell apart when his daddy died, and his focus wasn’t on school. But I’m very thankful that you helped him. He wouldn’t have been happy not being with his friends.”

“Well, it wasn’t a problem at all, he really did a lot of it on his own and Maude helped a lot.”

“He is a very bright boy when his mind can focus on what needs to be done.” the teacher said.

Lance was usually not far from Ray, as though he wanted those last few moments with his friend. Several people stopped in to wish Ray well on his journey to wherever the road took him. Mrs. Johnson, Lance's neighbor lady told him, "You know, that man stopped by the other day, the one that you run off with threatening to turn him in." She pause and Ray had a brief feeling of dread that Hope had let the man back into her life, but the woman continued. "Strangest thing happened, he got out of his car and that dog of theirs went full on attack mode on the man. He chased him right back to his car and stood there and growled at the man until he drove away." She wished Ray well on his travels and walked away.

"That's weird" Lance said. "Lucky's never been like that with anyone before. "I wonder if that's the man that scared him?"

"It might be, or it may just be that Lucky knew he wasn't a good man and didn't want him near your mom." Ray said. "He's become pretty protective of both you and your mom."

"Yeah, he's definitely our dog." Lance agreed.

Ray noticed Sally sitting at the booth in the corner watching the festivities. She had her staff working to serve everyone although it wasn't a full menu, they had some finger foods and cookies and cupcakes. But the servers would get beverages as needed. He walked over to talk to her. "How has it been not having an energetic child in the house anymore?"

"It's been lonely." Sally said. "I never knew what I was missing until I had it and then lost it again. Lance still comes over, but the house seems so quiet."

"Is Steve still on the fence about having kids?" he asked.

"No, actually, we've decided to look into adoption or maybe foster care." Sally said. "I really don't think I want to try to run the diner while pregnant or with a new baby, and there are kids out there that could really use a good place. I think it's our best option."

"It's a great idea." Ray agreed. "I can put you in touch with a friend of mine in LA who works in that area. She can give you some input on how to get started at least."

"I'd appreciate that." Sally said. "You know when you first walked into my diner a few months ago, I was skeptical about who you were and why you were here, but you've changed this town in so many good ways. Thank you for finding us."

"Well, it was my pleasure to meet you all." Ray said. "I don't think I really did anything all that special, but I'm happy that I was able to play whatever part I had in it all."

When the farewell party was winding down, and most people had left, Hope took her turn at thanking Ray. She walked to where he had been sitting and sat across from him. "I know there are no words to tell you how much I appreciate what you have done for me. You helped me get my life back and redeem myself as a mother. I know I would have lost Lance if you hadn't worked so hard to keep this out of the legal system. I could have gone to jail and he would have been taken away from me. I would have had to fight to get him back and that may not have ever happened."

"Mrs. Johnson told me that your old dealer tried to stop by." Ray said. He wasn't sure she had even known that.

"He did." Hope said.

"She said that Lucky chased him off." Ray said. "Lance thought that was odd because the dog has never seemed aggressive."

"No, Lucky wasn't aggressive until I told him to attack and opened the door." Hope said with a smile. "I didn't know if the dog knew the command, but I was hoping he would at least scare Tommy off, and he did."

"So you knew he was there." Ray said.

"I did, and I wanted him to know he's not welcome to come back." Hope said. "Although he probably thinks I still owe him money."

"No, I took care of that the day I took pictures of his license plate and his face in case I ever needed to turn him in." Ray said.

"I'll repay you." Hope said.

"You pay it forward by being the best mom you know how to be and by promising me you'll call Kelly if you ever feel like you're too overwhelmed."

"I will, the meetings help though." Hope stated. "And Sally and Steve are always there to lend a hand if I need a break or if I'm just feeling like a failure."

"You're definitely not a failure." Ray encouraged. "You had a horrible situation to deal with. You're not the first person to ever turn to drugs when it seems like life is too much to deal with. You have the tools now to cope, and you have a support system with you family and Maude. Lean on them, and please, call me if I can ever be any help with anything at all."

"I will. Thank you." Hope said. She went back over to talk to Sally and Lance walked up to Ray.

"I wish you didn't have to go." the boy said.

"I know, but you've got your mom and Lucky to be with you now." Ray began. "And you know you can call me anytime your mom says it's okay. You have Maude to go to if you need help with homework. Sally and Steve will be there for you too, anytime you need them. I'll be back to visit. I don't know exactly when, but I'll be back."

Lance wrapped his arms tight around Ray's waist and held on for a long time. Ray held on too. Despite the fact that he really did want to see the country, there was a part of him that wanted to stay right here with these people. He had made connections that he would never forget. And he knew he would check back in often either by phone or video chat. He had already made arrangements with Maude for him to be able to keep in touch with Hope and Lance by letting them use her tablet.

He walked with the two out of the diner and knelt down to say his goodbyes to Lucky too. "You take good care of them, boy. You watch over them and protect them and you be a good dog and rely on them for all the love and care you need."

He got into his SUV and drove to Maude's for one last sleep and one last breakfast in the small town before making his way eastward to the next stop on his journey.

# Epilogue

Ray had been driving for about five hours when he decided it was time to find a place to grab a bite to eat and get out and stretch his legs. He wasn't far from his next destination, the Grand Canyon. He would ask at the restaurant if there were any hotels or bed and breakfasts nearby. He ate his meal and while he was standing at the cash register waiting for someone to come and take his payment, he noticed a small bulletin board. There was a sign that said 'Free Room and Board in exchange for handyman.' There was an address and a phone number. Something in Ray told him this was his next stop. He wasn't a carpenter or anything, but he had done most of his own upkeep and repair on his home over the years. He would at least stop by and see what all they were wanting in exchange for the room and board.

The waitress had given him directions to the address on the paper. He was watching the house numbers looking for the right one, when he spotted what looked to be a man about a hundred years old on a ladder. It looked like he was trying to clean his gutters. There was no way Ray wasn't going to try to intervene. His conscience wouldn't let him. He could just imagine the nightmares he would have picturing this old man falling off that ladder and breaking something or worse. He parked on the side of the road and approached the man, he didn't want to startle him too badly because that might make him fall too, but he wasn't sure how to get his attention. Nature took care of that for him when he stepped on a twig he hadn't noticed on the ground and it snapped under his weight. The old man turned to see what had caused the sound.

"Hi." Ray began. "Are you by chance the one looking for a handyman?"

"I am" the man said. "Are you looking for work?"

"Well, I guess that kind of depends." Ray said. "I'm not a carpenter or plumber or anything, but I have done most of the upkeep on my house in the past."

"I don't need anyone with too many skills." the man said. "Mostly just cleaning the gutters, mowing the lawn. I got some boards that need replacing and some things that need painting. I would do it myself, but I'm not as young as I used to be, and my legs just ache sometimes."

Ray held out his hand and said "I'm Ray. I'd be glad to take a look and see if they are things that I think I can handle."

The other man shook his hand and said "I'm Dick, Dick Mitchell. You needing a place to stay, Ray?"

"I do." Ray admitted. "I'm going to be taking some pictures of the canyon and I need a place to land for a while. I'm not on any set schedule, so I can drive up and take pictures in between things you need me to do around here."

"Well, come on in then." the old man said. "I'll show you around."

Ray felt like maybe he had found his next adventure along the way. If he could help this man not have to be on a ladder again. He would gladly stay and do so.

## About Author

Riley Dawson is from Michigan and has been writing in various genres for several years. Her grandfather wrote poetry around the time of the Great Depression and the New Deal. Riley never met her grandfather, but apparently the writing bug transferred to her anyway.

In 2021, she found a friend that inspired her to write a series about paying it forward and this series came to be.

She spends her free time taking care of her elderly parents and babysitting two of her grandkids.

Made in the USA
Columbia, SC
03 June 2022

61245867R00102